An Order of Coffee and Tears

a novel

BRIAN SPANGLER

ISBN: 978-0-9852255-2-0 (eBook)
ISBN: 978-0-9852255-3-7 (print)

Editing by Mikaela Pederson
mikaela@a-step-up-editing.com

Editing by Don Shope
dshope100@gmail.com

Cover art by Streetlight Graphics
http://streetlightgraphics.com

DEDICATION

To my friends and family for their support and patience.

ACKNOWLEDGEMENTS

While working on this novel, there were several who I owe a terrific level of gratitude and appreciation. Thank you for reading many drafts of the novel and for offering critiques and encouragement – your feedback has helped to shape the story. Gabby, Ms. Potts, Suzette and all the rest, thank you too.

To Monica Spangler, Jenn Steiger, Susan Spangler and Jenn Bell for providing terrific feedback and helping me recognize the potential of the story.

To Don Shope and Evelyn Shope for reading later drafts and providing outstanding story suggestions and edits.

To Kay Bratt – A special thank you for all the time and support you gave in contributing and helping make this novel what it is.

1

Miserable Mondays – that is what I called days like these. Gray skies, northeast winds, and a cold damp bite on your skin. Thick sheets of rain drummed against the glass front of the diner where I worked as a waitress. Through the red letter print of Angela's Diner, the outside view of cars and buildings was a lively blur, stretched and pulled by the rainfall.

I missed Texas. Home. Sure, it had its share of cold wet days, but with the warm gulf air, you rarely ever felt the chill. Big-city air is different. The chill here reaches your bones and sometimes just settles in for the season. Philadelphia, the city of brotherly love (not sure why they call it that) is the city I called home now – has been for the last year, anyway. Angela's Diner is what folks liked to call a 'throwback.' *A welcome carry-over,* some of my regulars said. I was told the small restaurant was an original Jerry O'Mahoney Dining car that had been bumped out years before. Who built the diner and where it came from wasn't much of a concern – at least not when I first came upon it. Homeless and hungry, the *Help Wanted* sign in the window was all that mattered to me – well, that, and the smell of food escaping the door.

My name is Gabriella Santiago, but only my mother calls me Gabriella. To everyone else, I'm just Gabby. I didn't grow up wanting to be a waitress. I doubt most of those who wait tables do. Home for me was growing up in the heart of Texas – the heart of country. There I lived with my Daddy and Momma, who were as vanilla average as the houses on our street. Good people. Good family. And, like my home, I was a typical teenager. I dressed my bed with stuffed animals, like other girls. I taped posters on my walls, like other girls. I even let Tommy Grudin go to second base with me while playing a game of truth or dare, like other girls.

There was a time when I had more about me to tell, but who I was once is only a glimpse of who I am. Much of my past is a blur – most of it, from my own doing. Somewhere between that first kiss and cheerleading tryouts, I lost my way. I left home in a run and never looked back. I'm twenty-six now, and a lot of things have happened since the day I felt Tommy Grudin's eager fingers fumbling beneath my sweater. From time to time, I think about that part of my life – usually, though, I stay in today, since that is all we really have.

Closing my eyes, I listened to the eerie voice of the diner. A hollow emptiness. I found it unsettling. I forced a memory of the diner as I'd first seen it, like a carnival put up in a groomed field, it was bustling and beautiful. My eyes were lost in the silvery steel, and the shades of green panel decorations, and the neon lights glinting off the glass. I think I might have giggled. In fact, I'm sure of it. The diner looked out of place next to the modern buildings. Almost as though someone forgot it was there, and built an entire new city around it. Maybe that was the appeal it had. Maybe that's why it looked so warm and full of life and persuaded me to want to go inside.

When I opened the diner's door that first time, the smell of coffee and waffles and chicken and everything else that is good to eat hit me like a cozy breeze. Inside, the diner was abuzz with sounds and sights of dishes and dinnerware clanking, people laughing and talking. With nearly every seat taken, the booths along the windows were full. Children played with the mini-jukeboxes at the end of their tables as their families stirred coffee and sipped at milkshakes from tall fountain glasses. Round metal seats with greenish-yellow vinyl tops sprouted up through the floor like dandelions in spring. Two counters, separated by an old mechanical cash register, were covered with the perched elbows of folks dining alone. While the memory was fleeting, it was good and it warmed me inside.

That *Help Wanted* sign saved my life. I know that sounds odd, but it's true. I'd pulled the sign from the window and handed it to a hard looking waitress, whose name tag read, Ms. Potts. I remember how she shifted her feet and punched her hand to her hip before giving me a long stern look. When her eyes fell to my Chuck Taylor sneakers they stayed there. I was on the streets back then and my sneakers were thready, tattered and worn, much like me. And I remember the self-conscious pinch of embarrassment in my gut as I pulled one of my feet behind the other. A small miracle happened then: Ms. Potts kept the *Help Wanted* sign and Angela's Diner kept me. Miracles aren't always a grand happening like the kind I learned about in Sunday school. Sometimes they're as small as giving someone a break. I went into the diner that night, and since then, my life has never been the same.

Ms. Potts and I work the three-to-three shift most every day. We're a good team, but admittedly it didn't start out that way. I wasn't just bad. I was terrible. I didn't know a bus-pan from a black and white, or a pick-up from a clean-up. There is patience, and then there is whatever it is that Ms. Potts is made of. Unlike me, she is younger than some and older than most. But that doesn't stop her from running the place, something she's been doing for a very long time.

Ms. Potts sat across from me, working a crossword, and seemed to be oblivious to the empty diner and heavy rains. She huffed an objection to a word she'd penciled and then stabbed an eraser at the paper. Her blue hair was home to a few more pencils, and her biggish glasses sat perched near the tip of her nose as she scratched a new word into the paper boxes. Turning toward the back of the diner I expected to find Clark's large silhouette, his broad shoulders moving as if in a dance while he worked the grill to fill orders. But there were no orders. None. Clark's figure was absent and I thought he might be snoozing on his cot. He had a small bed, which was cramped into the back room; a small area that was all his. When he wasn't working the grill or helping clean the front, or doing anything else, you'd find him back there sometimes reading, sometimes praying, and most times sleeping.

Listening past the rain and wind hitting the window, I could hear the soft static hisses and pops of the Jeopardy game show theme song. It was Clark's portable black and white RCA Television. On the best of days, that little TV could get eight channels. Today, my guess was that the Philly locals were the limit: stations like three, six, and ten. And from the sounds of it, even Jeopardy was fading in and out.

5

Earlier, we'd seen a couple of our regulars who were off to their night jobs for the evening. For the day, I counted just a few dollars in my waist apron and felt the round imprints of a quarter, maybe two. When you work at a diner, your tip money, more often than not, might be the same change you're giving back. *When it's time to lean, it's time to clean,* I heard in my head – a favorite saying of the owner. And this diner was clean. Washed on the inside, and, squinting a look through the ever-changing mural of our front window, it was clearly washed on the outside, too.

When I turned back to check the progress on the crossword, Ms. Potts was looking at me. No, she was staring. The interest she had in her puzzle was lost. Maybe she'd come across a word she didn't know, or maybe she'd finished it. But then a few seconds passed. And then a few more. Uneasiness settled in me and I shifted in my seat. Uncomfortable. Who likes to be stared at?

A heavy wash of rain hit against the window, pulling my eyes away from Ms. Potts. I saw a few blurred and distorted rain parkas, and some umbrellas racing by the diner. One of the umbrella figures, a bright yellow that stood out loud against all the gray, slowed, and then stopped. *A customer*, I thought, and got ready to stand. But the yellow umbrella figure adjusted something, and then continued walking until it disappeared into the heavy weather. When I turned back to face Ms. Potts, she was still staring.

For a moment, a terrible thought crossed my mind. I thought that maybe Ms. Potts had died – right there across from me. She'd had a heart-attack, or a massive stroke, and the last thing she'd seen in this world was me. I didn't move. For another moment, I didn't move. But then the thought of her dying started to become more real, and I leaned in a bit as concern for her grew. When she blinked her eyes, I jumped. While it startled me, my heart lifted, as small relief settled in the form of a quiet sigh. The good thing was that I knew she was okay. But she continued to stare. Finally, I raised my eyebrows and shrugged my shoulders.

"What is it? Do I have something on my face?" Her stare broke.

She put her hands back on the table, and asked, "Girl, how long you been here?" Her expression remained fixed and stroke-like. I waited to see her display that familiar smile, or to see her fix her glasses before they slid too far down her nose. But she didn't do either. And I think I knew where she was going, and that made me more uncomfortable than her staring had. This time, I didn't have to let the heavy rain against the window pull my eyes. I forced myself to turn away from her and watched as a few who braved the harsh weather passed by the diner.

"Gabby? Hunny, I'm just asking a question," she began in a softer, but more inquisitive, tone. "You've been with us a year, and I ain't never heard you say a word about family. We all got some family... somewhere. But never a word," she finished.

"But you're my family. You and Clark."

"Sure, sure – we's family. But what about your own mother and father? You say they alive, you just never talk about 'em. They're your family, Gabby. And I'm sure they miss you. I know I would."

This wasn't the first time Ms. Potts had questions for me. She'd wondered before, and asked a few times. And, as before, I didn't like it. What's in the past stays in the past. By now, I'd shared where I was from, and that I hadn't been home or in touch with my parents in a long time.

Almost ten years had passed since I'd talked to anyone from my hometown. Ten years. That's double digits. I'd never considered that length of time until now. I was just sixteen when I left. Leaving wasn't a decision that came lightly. Leaving wasn't even a question or consideration I had that morning. I can still remember waking up in my old room that day, my dog at the end of my bed, the warm sun on my face, and the feeling of the comforter that I'd rolled myself up in. By that afternoon, all of our lives had changed forever, and, by the time the sun was setting, I knew I had to leave. There was no question. As the day ended, Texas grounds were under my feet for the last time, and I never looked back.

Before I could stop it, before I could control it, before I even really knew it had started, I was crying. And I was mad. Mad at Ms. Potts for driving me to cry in front of her. Mad at her for digging again. Mad that she was looking for something that I'd buried. I had buried my past a long time ago. I'd buried my memories, and the people in them, too. And what people choose to bury should always stay buried.

"Oh, baby, I'm sorry. I just want to know what happened, is all," she said, reaching across the table to hold my hands. I didn't pull my hands back. I wanted to, but I didn't. I couldn't remember the last time someone had held my hands, or even touched me. Had it been ten years? Surely it couldn't have been. It was this last thought that got me crying again. I just shook my head no, no, no, and fixed my eyes on Ms. Potts, pleading for her to not dig anymore. Not now. Not yet.

"Okay, baby. I understand. Gabby, I ain't never had no one to call one of my own, but I come to think of you as close as I'll get. I love you, girl – just want what is best for you," she finished, and rubbed my hands in hers. I pushed a breath out and felt a shudder from a tear as it went cold on my cheek.

When I was ready, I asked, "Why? Why do you need to know?" Ms. Potts stopped rubbing my hands. Her mothering eyes changed. She turned in Clark's direction, and then back to me, her expression now stale and flat.

"Because, Gabby, I know how your past can drive you. Drive it every damn day God wills you a breath to live. I know it," she said, and squeezed my hand.

It was my turn to look to Clark, but he was still in the back, watching his little TV. Ms. Potts pulled on my hands. She took my chin in her fingers so that my eyes met hers.

"Listen to me, girl, you gotta face your secrets. Secrets ain't free – you gotta face 'em, or else you gonna be running from them the rest of your life," she cautioned. And that is when I knew, I knew in my heart that my new home, my new family – they had secrets, too.

2

"Order of coffee and tears!" I called out when a familiar sight caught my eyes. I'd first met Suzette Wilkerson about a year ago. It was an early winter day much like today; with short afternoons and cold evenings, putting frost on everything as a reminder of what was to come. I remember that first day, not just because Suzette held her arm to protect two broken ribs, but because she was beautiful – in a delicate way. A waterfall of red hair played a perfect complement to her porcelain skin. Not quite reaching her mid-twenties, she held a striking pose that was tall and willowy. I recall yelling out for an order of coffee and tears, just as I had moments ago. And like before, Suzette looked out of sorts. No, she looked hurt.

My heart sank. All I could think was, *not again*. Her eyes were red and heavy with the same glassy tears this afternoon that had been there that first day. But today, she wasn't holding her arm to protect broken ribs. Today, I could see errant locks of hair stuck to the side of Suzette's face and her left cheek rising to a shine, a blackish-purple lump. The kind you get from the back of a hand. A man's hand.

Suzette paused before stepping up onto the sidewalk. She found me through the large glass window. Past the pock-mark remains of raindrops and the lettering of the diner's name, I watched as she tried to clear her eyes and push her lips into a smile. She struggled to fix her coat, which appeared to have been put on in a rush. Not just a rush, but a run from her home. She tried to hold her smile another moment, and even attempted a wave of her hand. But, when she began to tear up again, she let her coat fall open as she lowered her head and cried, defeated.

"Girl b-been hit again," I heard from behind me. "You can see it p-plain as plain from here," Clark went on to say, as he worked the diner's grill.

"Mmm-hmm. She needs to get away from that man," Ms. Potts followed. Pouring a cup of coffee, she continued, "How much the girl gonna take? It only get worse... never better." Without looking up, Ms. Potts finished pouring, and turned to me with hard eyes, "It ain't never gonna get better," she concluded in a stern voice.

"I know," I nodded and waved for Suzette to come in before she completely broke down. Suzette pulled the front of her coat closed and hurried to the door. The bell above the diner's entrance rang once as the smell of damp December air followed her inside.

"Hi, Gabby," Suzette struggled to get out.

"Not a word, hunny – just sit a spell," I offered. But I could see she needed to talk. She needed to spill the bad that had happened to her so that the good left behind would make her feel better. I did the only thing I knew to do for her: I fixed her a cup of coffee. By now, I knew just how she took it.

Pushing my hand across the counter, I offered Suzette a napkin. When she looked up at me, I motioned a circle around my mouth. A small thread of blood crept from the corner of her lips and was threatening to travel toward her chin. Suzette was hurting. Probably more on the inside than the black and purple bruising showed on the outside. When I saw confusion and uncertainty in her eyes, I motioned with my hand again. A few of the diner's patrons were stretching their necks – their eyes strained and reaching to see what was going on with the woman who'd cried a flurry of words before heavy sobs settled in. I didn't want to pull any more attention in our direction.

Suzette nodded and fixed me a look full of humiliation. With her eyes watering, she ran the white linen over her trembling lip. She cleaned her mouth of the blood, which revealed a split in her lower lip. It was beginning to swell. Ms. Potts pulled another napkin and filled it with ice. The chunky sound of ice cubes thumped the counter as she placed it in front of Suzette.

"Need to get some ice on that lip – cool the heat that's pushing the blood to swell. Cold will help keep it from bruising you," Ms. Potts offered. Lifting the large frame of her eye-glasses, she glimpsed the purple and red skin rising around Suzette's eye, and continued, "Can't help much with the shine on your eye, though, but may bring down some of that bump."

Wiping more blood onto the napkin, Suzette cringed and said, "I'll never get used to the taste of blood." When she reached to pick up the ice-pack, Ms. Potts took Suzette's hand in hers and held it there. Suzette lifted her chin.

"Hunny – you shouldn't have to. Nobody should," Ms. Potts answered in a soft tone, and placed the ice-pack fully in Suzette's open hand. Suzette looked as though she'd start crying again, but then she caught one of the sobs and choked it away before lifting the ice to cradle her chin.

"I know..." Suzette started, and then stopped to settle the shudder in her voice. "He's not a bad man. Really, he's not. I can't even remember the last time..." she continued, but her voice faded and her stare dropped to the coffee in front of her. Ms. Potts raised her brow and shook her head. We'd heard the same before. Many times. At least a dozen times, in fact, during my last year of working at Angela's. I wondered just how many times Ms. Potts and Clark heard the same before I joined them.

There was always a pattern, and I knew what was next. Suzette was going to defend her husband, James Wilkerson. She'd tell us how it was her fault, or how his bad day was allowance enough to beat on her. She was going to try and explain it away. Just explain it away with words she assumed were acceptable. No more questions. No concern. But we couldn't do that. We never could. We'd listen and console, and, time and time again, we'd give her the phone numbers of folks who could step in and help.

"How long?" I questioned. My voice pulled her eyes up from her coffee.

"What?" she asked. "How long for what?"

"How long since the last time he hurt you?" I repeated. Suzette shook her head, surprised by the question.

"A month, or more? Maybe?"

It was my turn to take Suzette's hand in mine. Her skin was cold, and her fingers were thinner than they should have been. I realized what I'd missed when she first came in, but now I could see it. She'd lost weight. Her skin was pale, her face tight against her cheeks. As anyone would do, my immediate thoughts were of sickness. A bug, or flu, or God forbid something worse. But then I considered how she lived day to day, every day. The anxiety that she carried inside her was like a hot stone that burned with the rise and fall of her husband's hand. Just the thought of how she felt inside when hearing the front door open made something stir inside me. It felt like fear, and an odd pressure turned my legs jiggly. *Anxiety is eating her up. How can she live like that?* I struggled to understand it, but couldn't.

Four marks, in the shape of flower petals, dressed Suzette's arm. They were the colors of autumn brown with threads of summer green. Only, the marks weren't the petals of spring flowers, they were the bruised places where her husband's fingers had gripped her. They were no more than a week old.

"And these?" I motioned, and then continued, "How does your shoulder feel? If I turn your hand over, will I find one more?" Suzette put on a frown and darted shame-filled eyes to Ms. Potts, then back to me. For a second, I was tempted to turn her hand in mine and reveal the larger thumb-print bruise, leaving nothing to question. Suzette pulled her hand back and tucked it away under the counter. *Please*, she asked with her eyes. Ms. Potts brought over more coffee and refreshed Suzette's cup.

"It's okay, hunny. It's okay. Just sit a while longer," she offered. And before I could say a word more, I saw, from the corner of my eye, a coffee mug hanging high above a booth. With fingers looped on the cup's handle, an older gentleman wearing a grime-stained *Keep on Truckin'* baseball cap motioned for some fresh coffee.

"Better tend to your table," Ms. Potts said, handing me the coffee. I turned back to Suzette and stopped. In that moment, a pang of guilt bit me as I considered how I must have made her feel. I didn't mean to make her feel worse. I just wanted her to see the truth.

"I'm sorry, Suzy – stay a while?" I pleaded. She nodded and pushed a smile, but then quickly reclaimed it as the swollen cut in her lip caused her to frown. When I reached *Keep on Truckin'*, he pitched his hat and lowered his cup.

"Ma'am," he said, and gave an appreciative look as I poured the coffee. He was a regular, and still called me "ma'am." A dozen times I'd told him he could call me Gabby, but he never changed his ways. I thought that was sweet.

"My apologies, and thank you for being patient," I said, and gave him one of my better *waitressy* smiles.

"No problem. I didn't want to call out, given the circumstances," he started, and brought the cup up to his lips. "Fresh smell of coffee got the best of me, though. Always will," he chortled, and sucked in the steam dancing just above his cup. Another sip, and he rested his cup back in front of him.

"Your friend gonna be okay?" he asked, his smile fading to concern.

"If we can get her to stay a while, then I think she'll be fine, and –" I never finished what I wanted to say. The bell over the door interrupted, sounding twice as the door opened, and then closed. Suzette didn't wait. She didn't stay. Another pang of guilt bit me, regret beginning to join it. I should have let the petal-shaped bruises go. I didn't need to prove a point.

When I looked over to Ms. Potts, she only offered a shrug of her shoulders. I'd hoped this time that maybe Suzette would have stayed. I'd hoped this time that she'd let us make some phone calls for her. I'd hoped – we'd *all* hoped – she wouldn't leave again, only to come back broken and sad, or possibly not come back at all.

Turning back to *Keep on Truckin´,* I finished, "I suppose we won't know, now."

"Shame, such a pretty girl, too," he started, and then picked up his coffee and continued, "I'll pray for her. We can do that much, can't we?" he said with a shallow smile. I returned a polite enough smile, but didn't want to. The regret was replaced by frustration, which was an all too familiar feeling. Walking back to Ms. Potts, I considered the past year. We'd see Suzette from time to time. Some visits came with smiles and talk of going back to school and moving on. Other visits were like today, where the bruises cried for her. How many times had

Suzette sat on the same stool, bleeding? How many times? *I'll pray for her. We can do that much, can't we?* I heard in my head.

3

"An order of coffee and tears!" Ms. Potts sang out, as the bell above the door rang, and echoed over our heads. A few girls – maybe thirteen or fourteen years old – pushed in through the door, and stood at the center of the diner. Shaking off the cold and a little snow, they clutched their arms in a hug to try and warm themselves.

We don't always call out "Coffee and Tears." I'd come to learn that we save that call for special occasions. Working at the diner from the late afternoon through the early hours of the next day, you see a lot of things. Some of them are funny, some sad. But most of all, you see those who, by chance, or by luck, find themselves at Angela's Diner, ordering coffee, and, soon after, crying. Might be a bad breakup, or a lost job, or even the death of a parent or child; we've seen and shared a lot of stories. I'd like to think of ourselves as the diner restaurant equivalent of a five-cent therapy. We'll give you the coffee, you supply the tears, and, in return, you'll get an ear that will listen.

I recognized the uniform the girls wore – dark maroon skirts that came all the way up and over white blouses with blue jackets dressed around their shoulders. The girls were from the all-girls school a block or so away. And, just a few blocks in the opposite direction was their partner school, the all-boys preparatory school. The two schools collaborated a few times a year to hold dances. As the only diner within a few blocks, we had the privilege of getting the school rush after the dances. On those nights, we'd need twenty hands to help us with the wall-to-wall teenagers swamping the diner. I'm not sure what the occupancy limit is for our little place, but we never counted. It was always work, but I enjoyed the kids. And I always felt a little sad when the night ended, as though I were trying to reclaim a little of something I missed.

Today was different. It was cold and rainy, and the shortest of the three girls looked to have been already crying a steady run of tears. She was a pretty girl with ruddy freckles across her nose to match her brown hair, and a row of braces I could see as she argued with the tallest of the three girls.

The tallest girl was the one they followed. She was the first to enter the diner and to pick a place to stand. I knew the type, and I think almost immediately that I didn't much care for her. Looking around the diner, she caught my eye, and I expected she'd give a nod for some seats and menus. But she didn't. And I thought there must be one more. As the leader of the group, she wasn't ready to sit down. There was someone they were waiting for.

The third girl, a red-head who I thought looked a little like Suzette, didn't seem to be engaged at all in the back and forth of the first two girls. Rocking on her feet, heel to toe, and gripping her school backpack, she seemed almost bored. Her eyes wandered around the diner with an interest in looking everywhere, but without looking anywhere. When the bell chimed and the door opened, number four came in to join the first three. Number four wore straight jet black hair, and if not for the loss of an inch or two in her height, she could easily have been the girl that the others followed. Soon after joining her friends, all four girls were together, and Blonde looked over to me and Ms. Potts.

"You want this one?" I asked, almost pleaded, with Ms. Potts. She gave the girls a quick look up and down, and then shook her head a stout "no."

"Coffee and tears is all that'll be there, fairly certain of it – I'm not up for teeny-girl storytelling. All yours, go get 'em," she answered.

"Really, are you sure? Are you sure you're not

interested?" I joked and laughed. But Ms. Potts held her face firm – eventually I saw a smile and heard a giggle as I picked up some menus and started walking toward the girls. By now, they'd selected their own booth and seated themselves. Or, should I say, Blonde did the seat selection, pointing out who should sit where.

"You sit here. And you sit there, and I'll sit here – of course, and, well... you can sit next to me," I heard her say as I approached.

"Afternoon, can I get you girls started with anything to drink?" I asked as I handed them each a menu.

"Four coffees, please," Blonde ordered for the group. Red, who looked the youngest, crinkled her nose and put on a face that told me she wanted something else.

"Is there something else I can get for you?" I asked, directing my words to Red. She raised her eyes and started to smile, but then turned in Blonde's direction. Blonde fixed a thinly veiled frown on Red, and while the glimpse lasted only a second, I recognized the power of it. Growing up, we've all had one of *those* friends. Black toyed with her hair, running long fingers through it, and snapped her gum, which cracked and popped as she chewed the air out of it.

"Oh, stop –" Black started, "How about four coffees and two chocolate milks? Please." Black gave Red a smile.

"That's fine – four coffees, *and* some chocolate

milk," Blonde followed in a tone that sounded condescending and mean.

"And two straws, please," Red insisted.

"Really? Again with the two?" Blonde scolded. Red straightened her shoulders defensively.

"Has to be two, otherwise the first one will be lonely." When Red finished her explanation, Black began laughing, and didn't seem to care that Blonde gave her a look that said to stay out of it. Black's lower lip pooched out as she shook squinted eyes at Blonde. I felt like I was going to start laughing right there – but I didn't.

"Can we get three chocolate milks?" the girl who was crying asked in a sparrow-like voice. I had to lean in close to hear what she asked when she repeated her order. Blonde rolled her eyes, and by then, I expected no less. Blonde passed another disapproving look around to the three other girls before her eyes settled on me.

"We'll have *four* coffees and *four* chocolate milks," she requested, a smile of her own breaking through. *I guess the truth is in the order.*

"I'm gonna mix some of mine together – like an iced mocha coffee," Red said to nobody in-particular, and giggled. "How about you, what are you going to do?" Red asked Brown, who'd already lost interest, and turned her eyes back to the table.

That is when the crying started again. Almost without pause, Brown began to bawl. Her freckles disappeared in the red that lifted through her cheeks. I looked over to Ms. Potts, but by now, she'd gone to the back to work with Clark, or watch *Wheel of Fortune* with him. And I wished I could, too. I'd seen my share of shed tears in the booths, but never from someone this young. I hated to admit it – I was nervous. There were no words that came to me. No wisdom or clever sayings. Nothing.

"I'll be back with your order," I heard myself say, and felt ashamed that I didn't say something more. Anything at all that might help Red. On days when Suzette would come to us broken and hurt, I felt that I knew what to say. I knew what to do. But this afternoon, I didn't know. Not a clue. As I began pulling together glasses of chocolate milk, Ms. Potts grabbed a glass to lend a hand.

"Poor girl's a mess. So, is it a breakup? Ditched by a boy? What's the story?" she asked, her eyes eager to hear more, as though this were an afternoon soap we never got to watch. After all, it was Clark's portable TV – game shows, and sometimes a news show. Nothing more.

"I don't know, yet. She just started crying."

"Young girls. Could be anything. We was young once, too," Ms. Potts laughed, and then continued, "And you still is," she finished, and patted my back.

The crying slowed by the time I placed the glasses of chocolate milk and cups of coffee in front of the girls. Brown's cheeks were stained with tears that continued a steady flow, like the rains outside. Some of the tears fell from her cheeks onto the table, leaving behind tear craters that reached out in every direction. I watched as one fell onto her school uniform, where it disappeared into the blue tweed of her jacket.

"Hunny, you okay?" I asked. While the order might have been the usual coffee and tears, the chocolate milk was indeed a better fit. Through the sobs, Brown was eagerly sucking down the chocolate milk. From my count, she saved only a sip or two for the coffee.

"We don't *know*," Blonde jumped in. Her voiced was gruff and meant to sound annoyed. "None of us know what's going on, do we?" she continued, almost reprimanding Brown for not telling them why she was crying.

"Really?" Black and Red pitched their voices, berating in near unison. "When she wants to tell us... *if* she wants to tell us, then she will," Black finished, and pitched up her coffee cup in my direction, asking for more. Unlike her friend, Brown, Black was enjoying the coffee.

Curiosity was getting the better of me, and I didn't want to leave before hearing what the story was. From the amount of crying, I was already guessing it had something to do with a boy. From the rain pelting the front of the diner's window, to Clark's shuffling of spatulas, pots, and pans, Angela's is a small diner, and sometimes, thankfully, the sounds carry to all corners. As I turned for the coffee pot, Ms. Potts was already standing by my side, coffee pot in hand.

"Coffee?" she asked with a smile that I thought spoke more of genuine interest and curiosity than it did politeness. Ms. Potts winked at me. She wanted to hear the story, too.

"Thank you," Black started to say, but then the tears interrupted again, and Brown's face turned to a mess that she pushed into the palms of her hands.

Blonde leaned up in her seat, and yelled, "You see? This is what she's been doing all day. And she won't tell us what's wrong." Ms. Potts raised her hand and motioned a polite "settle down."

Brown dropped her hands hard onto the table. Coffee cups jumped and spilled over, spoons rattled in their empty chocolate milk glasses.

"I'm pregnant, OKAY?" Brown hollered, and pushed her face back into her hands.

I jumped along with the other girls when I heard Brown yell. And when I realized what she'd said, my heart felt heavy, and I thought it skipped for a moment, while I tried to catch a breath that wouldn't come. Suddenly, I had a memory from a lifetime ago, but it passed as Ms. Potts moved forward to kneel next to Brown. Her knees sounded a loud pop as she made her way down so their eyes were near level. I remained standing. By now, I had the coffee pot in my hand and had refreshed each cup, whether the girls needed it or not. I wasn't leaving.

"Girl, are you certain?" Ms. Potts asked, as she laid her hand on the young girl's back.

"Yes... well, *I think* I am. Jimmy thinks I am, too, and now he won't even talk to me," Brown struggled to say, as a stutter of air caught her words. All the girls were listening now. Red stayed busy, her lips pursed on the two straws as she pulled more chocolate milk from the glass. Blonde and Black both exchanged sweeteners and creamers for their coffee.

"Wait," Blonde started to say. She put her coffee down and leaned forward. "Jimmy? Jimmy who?" All motion and sounds stopped as Brown sat as far back against the booth's seat as she could. Her face emptied of expression, and the red in her cheeks disappeared. She gave an undecided nod and pushed her eyes down to the coffee she'd left to go cold.

"*My* Jimmy?" Blonde squealed. Red quickened the emptying of her chocolate milk, and, for a moment, I thought her eyes were going to fall out of her head. Propped up on her elbows, Black cradled her coffee in her hands. She disguised an eager smile behind her cup as she listened to her friend's revelation.

"Jimmy Taylor," Brown finally whispered.

"Really? I mean, really!" Blonde scolded, and

slapped the silverware and coffee cups into another dance atop the table.

"I'm so sorry. I am. Jimmy said you and him were broken up, and then he called me, and then we started to hang, and then..." Brown stopped mid-sentence and began to tear up again.

"And then what? What? What happened?" Red's excited voice blurted in anticipation.

"We DID it!" Brown shouted. "Okay? Or, we sorta did it," she told her friends. By now, Blonde was fighting a tear. She held a narrow and hurtful stare on Brown.

Ms. Potts shifted on her feet and raised her hand again to quiet the girls. When all that we could hear were the sounds of the rain hitting the window, and Red's sucking down the last of her chocolate milk, Ms. Potts asked,

"Girl, do you mind if I ask you something? Might help. Might not." Brown darted looks around the table, and then nodded an okay. Ms. Potts blinked an acknowledgment, and continued, "Can you whisper in my ear what you and this Jimmy Taylor *did* do?" Brown hesitated. She searched the faces of her friends. First, she looked to Red, and then to Black, and, finally, she looked to Blonde. Her friends wore expressions filled with sympathy and fear and excitement, much excitement – except for Blonde. Brown leaned closer to Ms. Potts, and cupped her hand around her mouth and confessed. But with this confession, there wouldn't be the reciting of seven Lord's Prayers and ten Hail Marys as part of washing away your sin. Instead, just the smiles and laughs of Ms. Potts.

"Girl, you fine. Now, don't get me wrong. You young, your boyfriend young, and you both shouldn't be doing anything more than hand-holding, and maybe some kissing."

"I'm not pregnant?" Brown asked, a smile breaking free for the first time since she entered the diner.

"Girl, you're not pregnant. But I do expect you to have more explaining to do with your friends." Ms. Potts finished, and turned a hand to me to help her up. Her knees popped a few more times, but it was her laughter that caught my attention. Brown turned back to her friends, whose eyes were hungry for the details of their friend's near-pregnancy experience with one Jimmy Taylor. Brown's smile faded when she turned to Blonde. There would, indeed, be some details to explain, possibly over more coffee and chocolate milk.

"So, what was it?" I had to ask. But Ms. Potts didn't stop walking until we were in the back with Clark. Once we reached Clark, she let out a hearty laugh and clapped her hands together.

"They was just fooling around – nobody gonna have a baby with what they was doing. Poor girl naive about the *birds and bees,* is all, there's always one who is. Truth is, poor Jimmy Taylor gonna get both his ears chewed up once those two girls are done with him." Ms. Potts belted another laugh, and then turned back with me to look at the table. Black and Red were wide-eyed and listening to Brown and Blonde, going back and forth about a boy named Jimmy Taylor.

I tried to laugh, along with Ms. Potts. I did. I tried to hear the humor in it all, but the fright and terror I had heard in Brown's voice, and had seen on her face... well, it hit home. Seeing Brown this afternoon scratched a memory bubble that had been buried long ago. Memory bubbles can surface. I was sure I'd pushed it deep enough. I was sure of it. But, I suppose, nothing stays buried forever.

4

Ten minutes. It had been more than ten minutes since Ms. Potts walked to the back to have a discussion with the owner of Angela's Diner. This wasn't just odd, it was downright curious. We only saw Mr. Thurmon a few days a month, and usually those days fell on Friday. This was Wednesday. While I continued working tables, Clark kept to the grill and called out pick-up after pick-up. I kept my eyes on what I was doing, and on the orders I was taking, but I have to admit that the work was more of just a distraction. I wanted to know what was being said.

When I could, I'd walk across the diner so that I could spy a glance to the back room with the hopes of seeing what was happening. Passing by a few times, I found Ms. Potts and Mr. Thurmon exchanging words. And on one pass, Ms. Potts caught me mid-stride and shooed me away, her face scrunched with annoyance as the sound of the towel in her hand whipped at the air. Clark seemed impervious to it all. Not one time did I see him looking over his shoulder, or trying to lean in with his ear. Not a care – nothing. I suppose I was just curious enough for the two of us; that is what I told myself, anyway.

During our shift, we ran the diner, but we didn't own Angela's Diner. Angela Thurmon was the original owner. And from what I've been told, she built and breathed the diner after her husband died. It was her baby. She said she built Angela's because she wanted to work something good and steady. She said that if there is a business to spend your days working, then you might as well pick one everyone needs. I never gave it much thought when Ms. Potts explained it, but now I realize everyone does need to eat. How many times have you walked by a restaurant only to stop and then step in for a quick bite? I know I did little more than a year ago. I just never left.

My boss is Angela's son, Thomas Thurmon. I've heard Ms. Potts call him Junior. He grew up in the diner. Back then, mommas couldn't drop their babies off at a day care, afford an all-day sitter, or hire a live-in Au Pairs. And in Angela Thurmon's case, she was a single parent with two babies to tend to: the diner, and Junior. So, Junior spent his days playing in the diner. I imagine there could have been worse things.

All things considered, I think Junior must've had it pretty good growing up with his days spent in Angela's Diner. I can picture him in my head, running around and playing under the booths, his makeshift hideaways. Or maybe snaking through the stool posts at the counter, probably imagining them as steel pillars – a gateway to some mystical land. Maybe he had a toy car, or something, and, with it, he made traveling mysteries and adventures. He could've used the sounds of the diner with busy trucks passing on highway overpasses, their heavy traffic sounds filling the diner and staying true to rush hour. A quick glance around the diner, and I laughed at the child-proofing that would have been called to question today.

Ms. Potts knew Angela Thurmon better than perhaps anyone. And there was never a shortage of stories. Angela had lost her husband at a young age to a horrible car accident involving a drunk taxi driver. Newspapers followed a big public outcry against the taxi company, which was one of the largest and richest in the city. Talk of scandal and cover-up ended with a handsome settlement paid to Angela and Junior. The settlement was enough that Angela never had to work again – she could have easily spent her days minding Junior and doing whatever else pleased her. Instead, she put all her money into the diner and into the land the diner was sitting on. She had straight up ownership of it all with only the monthly food bills, maintenance, employees, and utilities as the overhead – nothing else.

Ms. Potts happened to be one of her first employees. Clark followed a year or so after. Angela filled her days working to make the diner successful. No job was too big or too small. She worked the grill alongside Clark, waited tables, or cleaned the bathrooms when the need wasn't filled quickly enough for her taste. She worked all the jobs, even repaired the roof after spring winds opened it up like a tin can under hungry fingers.

When arthritis put a limp in her step, it slowed her some, but not enough to stop her. This was her place. As she grew older, the arthritis moved from her hips and legs, to her feet and hands. Soon, the simple jobs, the basic ones, were too much. A stool at the cash register became her last station. Most days, she'd greet folks and chat up a hello and goodbye, followed by a whispery *please come again*. But her diner out-lived Mrs. Angela Thurmon. She'd grown ill, and the arthritis aged her more quickly than she should have. And then there came one afternoon. The sun was setting, and Ms. Potts said she saw a tear in Angela's eye as she told Junior that she thought it was time for her to go home. Ms. Potts told me she often wondered if on that particular day, Angela knew it would be her last day at the diner.

She died less than a month later. Ms. Potts said that a little piece of Angela's Diner died the day they put Mrs.

Thurmon in the ground. Junior was already grown, and now a well-respected lawyer in downtown Philadelphia. He cared and supported a family of his own. He brought them to his mother's diner from time to time, which always pleased Ms. Potts. He made sure Ms. Potts and Clark stayed on. He'd kept Angela's Diner. He'd kept all of it.

I'd met Mr. Thurmon sometime during my first month of work. An attractive older man, he wasn't at all anything like I pictured him. Often, I'd hear Ms. Potts and Clark make light of Junior and some of his antics growing up at Angela's. But the man I met didn't fit the image. I suppose this is true for most of us. The cousins and the younger siblings of friends we grow up with end up completely different. The person they become is a mere shadow of the person you remember them to be. They're grown-up with adult lives and adult problems. That was Junior.

Mr. Thurmon's laugh is something, too – I think we'd all admit to enjoying it. Ms. Potts said it was Angela's laugh, as well. It's a very contagious laugh that almost always gets us all going when we hear it. When he'd get to talking about his time as a child in the diner and the games he'd play, he would smile and laugh, and maybe even glow a little; just enough for me to get a glimpse of the little boy Ms. Potts and Clark liked to talk about.

We never knew exactly when Mr. Thurmon planned to stop in. Fridays were payday. As waitresses, we earned an hourly wage, as did Clark, so there was something. Not much, but something. Other than Friday, I think his stopping in had more to do with being in the neighborhood, or a drop in with the kids to see Ms. Potts.

On this particular visit, he didn't come with paychecks in hand, he wasn't looking to get a bite to eat, or to pick up the receipts and books for the week. I could smell his aftershave follow him as he walked passed me. He offered me a polite smile and a hello, and threw another smile and hello to Clark, who replied with a brief nod from behind the grill. Ms. Potts was already in the back, which is where they've stayed. Some of the time, he'd stand with one hand stroking his necktie, and other times he'd talk as Ms. Potts listened.

All kinds of thoughts were going through my head. The biggest was that they'd have to let me go. I'd overstayed my welcome. My time at Angela's might be over. My newfound family would have to say goodbye. Angela's could be busy at times. Almost crowded. But it wasn't consistent, at least not as often as I saw the first months of working here.

Just a block away from Angela's Diner, a fast-food restaurant was put up, nearly overnight. One day, a group of construction workers showed up, wearing green-yellow reflective vests, and white helmets. With shovels and pick-axes in hand, they broke the sidewalk into pieces, digging up the ground, and making an awful noise that rattled the diner's front window. Within a week, it seemed, there were already lights on the inside of what they'd built, with palm-sized round bulbs twinkling a run along the pitched red roof outside. The same types of lights blinked around a bright sign that stood in front of the freshly manicured landscaping. The sign spelled out a 'Grand Opening' welcome, and some other nonsense I didn't read. I'd walked past the sign, stopped, and spun around to give it a once over. My first thought was Angela's Diner. When the doors did open, I think a bit of our business left. A big bit, or, should I say, a bite!

I've walked past the fast-food place every day on my way to and from the diner. Their parking lot is always full, and enough bodies are lined up to keep me from seeing through the wall-to-wall glass windows. It is a busy crowd. A fast crowd. A crowd interested in getting in and getting out. There are days when it is full of a younger group of kids. On those days, I've seen teens wearing blue tweed jackets and gray blazers. They're the kids from the all-girls and all-boys school. A few of the faces, I recognized, and even remember serving a coffee or two. Once, I glimpsed Blonde and Red, sitting atop a beige plastic booth, laughing it up with some boys while dipping fries into their chocolate and vanilla shakes.

"Hi, Gabby. Ms. Potts and Clark treating you okay?" Mr. Thurmon asked. I jumped when I heard his voice, startling the fast-food thoughts away. At some point, the conversation in the back of the diner broke, and, while Ms. Potts continued working an inventory check, Mr. Thurmon had poured himself some coffee and had taken a seat at the counter.

"Yes. Yes, thank you," I answered quickly, thinking my voice sounded nervous. I passed him the creamers and sugar, and asked, "And you?"

With half a smile, he nodded his head and then gave his mother's diner a glance, "Same... but same is good, right?"

"Sure thing," I answered back, this time my words sounded stronger. Sipping his coffee, Mr. Thurmon began to say something, but then hesitated. Ms. Potts joined me at the counter, and Mr. Thurmon stood and took a step toward the booths and stared. Moving to the far corner, he knelt down on one knee, looked beneath the table, and began to laugh.

"Ya know," he started, his finger pointing under the table, "I used to fit under there. Amazing. This place used to look enormous to me." He chuckled as he stood, and then spun a seat on one of the counter's stools. Lifting his arms like a conductor of an orchestra, he announced, "A kingdom with shiny gates coming up from the ground, and Clark, our Knight, and Guardian of the Grill." His eyes were wide as he described a strange land he'd made up and played in as a boy.

"Junior. It's gonna be okay." Ms. Potts said, her voice shaky. She stepped toward Mr. Thurmon and placed a hand on his arm. "It's gonna be fine."

Mr. Thurmon turned to face us, his expression lost thirty years in that moment, and briefly, I saw a little boy's eyes, and a little boy's smile.

"Can you fix me some of your hot cocoa... with the little marshmallows? It's been years since I've had your hot cocoa," he begged with his hands brought together.

"Sure thing. Would be my pleasure," Ms. Potts answered, and led him back to the counter where he took to his seat.

"Thank you," he said, his smile broad and his eyes wandering around the diner. Clark and I passed a confused look. I liked Mr. Thurmon. I didn't like seeing him like this. In fact, it scared me. Ms. Potts' expression told me it scared her, too. He reminded me of someone on the verge, someone who'd been given news that was just too much for them to take in one sitting.

Whatever he'd come to talk to Ms. Potts about, it couldn't have been good news. Selfish relief settled in me as I realized that any news this big couldn't have been about letting me go. Surely letting a waitress go due to financial reason wouldn't spin up Mr. Thurmon's cuckoo clock. That meant the news could be about Angela's

Diner, and that, too, wouldn't be good for anyone.

Ms. Potts hurried a cup of hot cocoa to the counter, and plunked three mini marshmallows into the small frothy pool floating on top. Steam circled above the cup, gesturing an invitation. My stomach growled, and my mouth watered. Ms. Potts held a proud smile. I think she rather enjoyed making Junior a cup of hot cocoa. For the minute or so of work, it probably took her back the thirty years I'd seen disappear from his face.

When his cell phone rang, his smile broke, and he quickly blinked away his childhood world. By the second and third ring, I could once again see the Mr. Thurmon I knew. The little boy was gone. He answered his cell phone, and within a minute, he was talking in a lawyer tongue none of us understood. He gave us a brief wave of his hand, and then left the diner – his cup of hot cocoa and marshmallows left untouched and alone on the counter.

The bell above the door rang an empty sound, and I couldn't wait to ask, "What was that all about?" But Ms. Potts didn't say a word. Not at first. Clark walked around the grill to the front to join me. Before answering, Ms. Potts took Mr. Thurmon's seat, picked up his hot cocoa, and drank down one of the mini-marshmallows.

"He's scared," Ms. Potts answered, her voice sounding unsteady.

"Ma'am, sc-scared of what?" Clark asked.

"My boy got himself a double today."

Embarrassed. I asked, "A double?"

"Double-bad. Junior hit twice with news nobody likes – ain't even six o'clock yet."

"Wh-what wrong with Junior, m-ma'am?"

"It's the arthritis, the bad one: the one that crippled his momma. The one that took her early," Ms. Potts answered, sipped the cocoa, and then whispered, "Took her too early. And now he got it. Gonna be a cripple, couple years."

From the stories Ms. Potts told, I could imagine the fear Mr. Thurmon must have been feeling. I felt bad for him, and thought it might have been why he came here today. He wanted to grab a taste of his days as a little boy, when his momma was healthy and they were happy. Ms. Potts said he got a double. What was the other news? I waited to see if Clark would ask, but he didn't.

"And the other news?"

Ms. Potts put her cocoa down and fixed her glasses, pushing them up with the tip of a finger. She looked to me first, and then to Clark, where she left her eyes, as she answered.

"Angela's is having some money issues. Coming in shorter than we were last year. With the news about his health, he's considering sellin' the restaurant."

"Is it the fast-food place?" I asked. I heard Clark sigh and watched as he rested heavily against the wall. Ms.

Potts stood up, her eyes still on Clark. She wiped at the counter. I could tell she was upset. She wiped the counter again and then stopped.

"Clark, you know what that mean?"

"Y-yes ma'am. I know." he replied and went back to the grill. Clark hung his head low, and his step was slow, as though the weight of the world suddenly found his shoulders. I was missing something. Selling Angela's Diner might just mean new owners. But I didn't think it was just the money. There was something else.

"We leaning, so there must be some cleaning," Ms. Potts said, and forced a smile. As I took to helping wipe the counter, Ms. Potts stopped, then sat back down to finish her cocoa. The same troublesome weight that settled on Clark's shoulders was visible in Ms. Potts' eyes.

5

Most weeks, the days at Angela's Diner tend to run together. While the faces of those coming and going may change, the looks in their eyes stay the same. And, if I'm not paying attention, then Mondays and Tuesdays just melt into Wednesdays and Thursdays. Maybe that is why some days stand out more than others. Maybe that is why some of the stories we hear at the diner stay with us for days, and sometimes longer. Friday is the exception. And, with money in their pockets, folks tend to shake off the last four days.

I work every day of the week, and sometimes on Saturdays. But I do have Sunday to call my own. After all, I have a room to tend to, and an agreement with Ms. Potts that I'd keep it respectable; somewhat, anyway. She is an easy enough landlord, and, I suppose, I am an easy enough tenant. Now, you'd think, with the two of us living under the same roof so to speak, that we'd see quite a lot of each other. But the truth is that I don't think I've ever crossed paths with Ms. Potts outside of the diner, except for when she handed me the keys to my new place. My heart skips a little each time I think about the sound of the keys as she placed them in my hand. I'd never had a place to call my own before – not one that was just mine.

Like I said, most days tend to run together. And then there are the days that stay with us when we go home. Some of them stay with us long after that. And others... they can stay with us forever. I can count on one hand the number of *forever* days. Don't even need all five fingers, just a few. Yes, a lasting impression.

The memorable days are the ones that seem to randomly play back in your head. No reminders or reasoning – it could be as simple as watering a house plant, like my Felix. Today was one of those days. I saw the faces and heard the conversations in my mind, and my poor Felix ended up with a little more water than he needed. I filled and spilled over the lip of the planter with some of his water and dirt running down onto the window sill. I'm sure Felix will survive.

I met an older woman today. Sandra – she said her name was – had stopped into the diner for some coffee to help pick her up during a particularly long drive. The drive was a fair distance, considering where she came from, and where she was going. A heavy smell of perfume carried with her as she took a seat across from me at the counter. As she settled, she thumped her purse onto the counter, and fished out a cell phone. There was a classiness in the way she dressed and carried herself, the kind you admire from afar. Maybe she ran the PTA, or had a seat on a council for her local community. Or maybe she dabbled in town politics, giving the up-and-coming politicians a run on their candidacy budgets.

A mature woman, I watched as she typed out a text message. Her painted nails sounded off a rattle of clicks and clacks as she pressed each of the tiny keys. She kept just a few rings on. There was her wedding band, and an engagement ring, and what looked to be an anniversary ring. And then I saw an odd silver ring that seemed out of place next to all the gold. If chance would have it, I thought I might ask her about the ring.

Sandra wore a shorter hair style than most women her age, for convenience perhaps, or maybe it worked better for her small, round face. Brown hair with sandy highlights, she cradled one side with her palm, and then the other, pushing back any strays that fell out of place. Grays were hidden away, but had grown out some. Maybe she'd missed a hair appointment, although she didn't strike me as the type that would miss one.

Diner instinct had my hands putting a coffee mug in front of her. Holding the pot of coffee up, I asked if she'd like a cup. I told her it was fresh, brewed just a few minutes ago. She returned a polite enough smile, and nodded yes. It didn't take long before I could see she was distracted. Her mind was someplace else.

"Thank you, dear. This is exactly what I came in for," she said in a voice that was soft, but clear.

Having noticed the wedding ring, I grabbed another cup for her husband. But, as I placed it down in front of the seat next to her, Sandra raised her hand and waved it away.

"My husband won't be joining me," she started to say, and then looked toward the front of the diner. "We parked up the street, and he made it half a block on our walk here. When he saw the bar across the way... well, I'll have the coffee, but he's decided to have something a little more spirited," she continued.

She turned back to me, her eyes empty, and with hushed words, she said the most curious thing. "He won't finish till he drowns it." I don't think she intended for me to hear what she said, and so she tried to smile past the comment with a short apology,

"Excuse me," she began, "just babbling."

"Not at all. So, are you and your husband passing through?"

"We're on our way to Delaware – started out earlier today from Connecticut a few hours back. We live up there half the year."

"Family? You have family in Delaware?"

Sandra stopped and considered the question. A smile bloomed on her face, and she answered, "We're going to pick up our boy. He's been overseas in Afghanistan the last eighteen months. Tom, that's my son – he's a hero."

I hated to admit it, but my knowledge of war and politics were vague at best. On occasion, Clark liked to fill me in on the details. But most of the time when I'd try to listen, I would lose interest in what he was telling me. Over the last year, I did get to know where I was, and who I was living with. Angela's Diner is in Philadelphia, and Philadelphia had a lot of its own going off to war. From what Ms. Potts had told me, quite a few of the young men were from our small neighborhood. Some came back. Some didn't. And a lot of them wished they hadn't gone over at all. This was the first mention of a hero, though.

The bell above the door rang, and a chill washed in far enough to reach me. Goose flesh danced over my arms as I tried to hug it away. The diner was nearly empty so I made use of the unfilled cup, and poured myself some of the hot coffee.

"A hero?" I asked.

"A hero," she boasted proudly.

"That really is something – you and your husband must be so proud."

Raising her eyes past me, Sandra's smile grew. She closed her eyes, put her hands over her heart, and mouthed his name. She finished her coffee and motioned for more before continuing.

"Oh, we are. Odd thing is, growing up, Tom really wasn't into the army thing, or cops and robbers, or any of that. I mean, he played the same video games, and maybe some play wars with the neighborhood boys. Other than that, he never showed an interest in the military." Sandra's eyes moved to her hands, and her eyebrows lifted slightly. "My son sided more with the creative – like this ring he made for me," she said, lifting her hand to show the silver band I'd wondered about.

"That is pretty – I was admiring it earlier," I commented. Sandra held the ring a second longer, but then her eyes narrowed, "It was his father. He watched the news all the time, and especially watched what was going on over there. You know, after 9/11. He was obsessed with it. I guess we all were, a little."

"I was just a kid back then. I remember seeing it at our school when it happened, and I remember our school letting us go home just before the second tower fell."

Sandra nodded her head yes, and said, "Tom's about your age. His school let out early, too. I suppose they all did when the towers were hit."

"So, is your husband in the military?"

Sandra hinted a smile and waved a dismissive hand,

"No, bad plumbing, is all. He wanted to enlist, and even tried once. A year before we started dating, he'd lost a kidney to cancer. *Easiest cancer to beat*, he likes to say. Things might be different now, but back then, you had to have both beans to enlist. Just having one wasn't good enough. I think they'd consider you a liability. Never really understood the reasoning. I mean, you only have one heart and one brain, right? So, his heart was always in it, and he wanted to, but he couldn't enlist."

"I can imagine how thrilled your husband must be for your son. I mean, being a hero, and all." At once, Sandra's expression went cold and hard. She gave her cell phone a quick lift to study the small screen.

"Yes. He is proud and thrilled – or he *was*," she answered, her voice sounded sterile and rehearsed. She dropped her cell phone back to the counter and looked up at me. "Sometimes I think maybe my son wouldn't have joined the army if his father hadn't talked about what was going on over there so damn much," she answered, her voice sounding callous. But then she shook her head and pushed a grin.

Sandra picked her purse up and raced through the contents. I thought she might be hunting down a photo of her son: the really nice military kind that people like to show off. Instead, she pulled out a letter. It was made up of formal stationery, and had an embossed emblem on the face of the envelope. Definitely military. Her eyes widened, and her face lit up as she asked,

"Can I tell you a story? Can I tell you how my son became a hero?"

At once, I was excited. The diner was slow, and getting a story was a real treat. "I'd love to hear it. Thank you," I told her, as she embraced the letter.

"This is just one of a dozen letters I've received from the men and women in his unit," she started, and then, for the next few minutes, Sandra told me how her son became a hero.

He was on patrol with his unit a few miles from their post, when they came upon a family standing in the middle of the road. A young woman was crying, and her husband frantically waved his arms at Tom's unit, begging for them to stop. They stopped, and one of the men stepped out to ask what had happened. The woman was beside herself; anguish took her words – all she could do was flail her arms and cry. The woman's husband was grateful Tom and his unit had stopped. He pointed out to the field next to the road where, they saw two kids playing. The soldiers quickly learned that the man and woman in the road were the parents of the two children. The mother cried out the same words over and over, and, finally, one of the men in the unit understood what she was saying. "Minefield," he barked loud enough for everyone to hear. By now, Tom's unit had filed out of their vehicles and lined up along the edge of the road. All of the soldiers stepped back from the minefield. One soldier had already trekked a handful of steps toward the children. The soldiers in the unit yelled for him to stop, and then talked him through repeating his steps, only backwards, until he was safely on the road.

Minefields are scattered across the Afghanistan provinces, Sandra told me. Most of them are blocked off with signs and makeshift fencing. Just about all of them are on a schedule to be demined. The minefield the kids wandered into was on the list, and was supposed to have been blocked off with fencing, but that never happened. Everyone in the area knew about it: the families, their kids. Everyone, except a set of curious twins. A boy and a girl, maybe five years old; old enough to walk and run, and young enough to not know any better.

Tom and his unit had no demining tools. A special group was usually called in to handle the clearing of a few mines, let alone an entire field. Personnel from the unit tried to explain this to the family – instead, the family continued their begging and pleading for help. They assumed that Tom and the others, given their military gear, could navigate the mines and save their babies.

The mother's crying slowed. The reports from the unit stated that she began to yell at her husband, hollering that he should be brave, that he should go get their babies. The father scolded her – his wife's words were considered disrespectful. Or maybe the father of the twins was ashamed, because he was afraid. The mother and father started to argue and yell. And maybe it was this disconcerting activity between the parents that caused what happened next.

The little boy stood up in the field and pointed to his mother and father. He stood up and began to say something in Afghani. His words were young, and new, and far too soft for anyone to hear from that distance. The little boy then pulled his sister up, and the two of them stood in the middle of the minefield, their attentions drawn in by their parents. They raised their voices and yelled to their parents, as children often do. They yelled to their mother and father, who continued to argue with each other. Tom was the first to see the twins lean into a step. It was a baby step, but it was a step, and there was no way to know where the land mines were buried. Tom ran to the mother and father, and instructed them to tell the twins to sit down and not move. But Tom's Afghani was new, too, and the parents were confused by his instructions.

By the time the twins took a second step, the other men and women in the unit saw the kids on the move, as well. They waved their arms up and down, motioning for the children to sit down. The twins must have thought it was a funny sight, all the helmeted soldiers in tan and brown fatigues, waving to them from the road. The children didn't sit down, they waved back. Laughing, they took another step.

"Sit down, sit down!" everyone began screaming. They continued waving their arms in the air. Tom raced through his Afghani/English translation book, trying to find the words. The twins weren't looking at their parents anymore. They were laughing at the site of the figures hopping up and down along the edge of the road. One of the reports stated that the little boy and girl started to jump up and down in a mimic, playing along with what they saw. When they grew tired of jumping, they stopped, and then took another step.

"*Ksséte, ksséte, ksséte,*" Tom yelled in Afghani to the children. He'd found the translation for *down,* and yelled it to the twins. The other men and women with Tom's unit did the same. The mother and father stopped their arguing. Their color had paled, and their faces grew sullen and scared. The little girl called out to her mother, her fingers stretched outward, gripping handfuls of air. And then they took another step.

The chanting stopped. Everyone sucked in a breath and waited. Nothing happened, and then the parents started yelling alongside the soldiers. They called out "*Ksséte, ksséte, ksséte,*" in a corrected pronunciation. And this time, the children heard them. The little boy argued that he didn't want to sit down, and that he wanted to come over to see the soldiers in their helmets and uniforms. He wanted to see if they had treats for them. His father directed him to stay. But the little boy shook his head, and, with his sister's hand in his, they took another step. A gust of wind pushed sand and dirt into the air. The winds stirred up a heavy cloud, hiding the twins from Tom's unit like a secret.

The men and women in Tom's unit waited: some raised their hands in front of their eyes, expecting the worst to happen. When the winds and dirt settled, and when nothing happened, they joined in with the father's demands. They stopped waving their arms and told the twins "down". A few in the unit radioed back to the base, seeking instructions. Any demining help would be hours past their need, which was immediate. The little girl jumped up and down, calling out to her mother. She pulled on her brother's arm, and they took another step. And then a second. And a third.

The unit's report stated that Sandra's son never hesitated. Tom didn't request permission, or wait to see if a mine exploded under the feet of the children. He just ran. He was half way to the little boy and girl before anyone realized what he was doing. Tom didn't try to jump to different points in the field – he didn't watch the ground where his feet landed. He just ran.

His entire unit began screaming at him to get off the minefield. Orders were shouted, calling out for him to discontinue and rejoin the unit on the road. But Tom heard none of it. He'd reached the twins, scooped up the boy like a football, and grabbed the little girl by her arm. When he stopped and turned back to face the road, he stood and searched the field of dirt for footprints.

"What are you doing?" Someone screamed out to him. They all knew what he was doing. If he hadn't run out to them, if he hadn't done something, then the twins almost certainly would have been killed. Tom's unit continued to yell and scream. They instructed him to find his steps and use them. Find his boot tracks, and follow them back out to the road.

The only sounds coming from the mother and father were prayers in whispered monotone words strung together in long breaths. They were kneeling on the ground, their hands brought together in front of them, pleading that Tom's tracks would be shown to him as clear as he could see their children. Tom paced his steps, and worked his way back to the road. At some point, the little girl began to slip from his hand. Tom tried to hoist her into his arms as he hurried himself, but her body fell from his fingers, and she tumbled hard to the ground. She cried and yelled something in Afghani at him. He tried to stop, but he couldn't. Momentum had his feet moving to the next boot track, and then another boot track, and then he was back on the road, dropping the boy and turning around. And the winds came again. The winds shouted louder this time, raising the dust and blinding everyone. More clouds of dirt and sand circled around the vehicles, the soldiers, and everything else, hiding the little girl whose cries were muffled by the sounds beating sands.

Tom was back to the girl a minute later – guided by her voice yelling to her mother, he ran and scooped her up in a tight embrace. The boot tracks he'd followed were gone, stolen by the wind. Reports state that Tom pulled the girl up in a hug, and simply raced for the road. He'd saved the twins.

Sandra's words were mesmerizing. I felt my heart racing, and it wasn't just the excitement of it, it was the pride. I could hear it in her voice. Amazing.

"You'll have to stop back in during your drive home – I'd love to meet your hero," I exclaimed, almost demanded, and beamed with a smile.

When the bell over the door rang, another chilly breeze fell inside the diner, as a balding man entered. His face was tired, his cheeks sunken. Dark gray pouches carried his eyes, which were blood shot and wet. He lifted his face just enough to see me and Sandra. Sandra turned, their eyes connected, and he gave a nod and walked toward us. When he reached the counter, he sat down. Tossing his keys to drop on the counter in front of him, he again lifted his chin just long enough to look at me.

"Coffee," he said in a voice that was gruff and broken. The smell of whiskey carried with him. I wrinkled my nose to the smell of it when he spoke.

"Sure thing," I answered, and poured the coffee. After a taste, he stood and told Sandra he was going to the restroom, and that he'd be back in a few minutes. He told her that they should get back on the road, that they had some hours left in their drive to Delaware. When he walked toward the restroom, I wanted to ask Sandra if he was okay. He didn't look as though he'd had one too many at the Irish pub down the street, but he didn't seem right. There was something more.

"That's my husband," she started to say. Picking up her purse, she fumbled through the contents and pulled out a tube of lip-balm. I thought she was going to cry as she squeezed some on her finger and rubbed it across her lips. Her expression changed for a moment, and she cupped her mouth and closed her eyes.

"I'm sorry," I whispered. "I don't mean to intrude... but is everything okay?"

Sandra opened her eyes, put a hand on mine, and blinked away a tear.

"My son is a hero. We're going to Delaware to pick him up today," she proclaimed. When she sat up, she cleared her throat and pulled back her hand.

"My son is a hero. He saved that little boy and that little girl. He ran out of that minefield, and missed all the land mines. Except that last one. The girl survived, but my son died two days later."

The local news stations in the Philadelphia area often cover what is going on in Delaware. It is there that you'll find the Dover Air Force Base, and a mortuary for the fallen soldiers returning home from overseas. I'd missed the connection. This wasn't a visiting trip to Delaware. They were going to Dover to receive their son.

"I am so sorry for your loss," was all I could think to say.

"Just wish I had another chance. Just one," she replied.

"Chance?"

"Tom enlisted to please his father. I know it. He wanted the approval," she started to say, her voice echoing in angry sarcasm. Shifting in her seat, she gave the restroom a hard look, as though she could see clear through the walls. "I blame him, you know," she continued.

"Ma'am, what your son did was an amazing and heroic thing." It was my turn to receive the hard look, and I thought I'd overstepped with my words. Her face softened and relaxed, and she nodded in silent agreement.

"If I could do it all over again, I'd stand up and

scream at Tom. I'd scream at them both, and say, listen, Mr. Thomas Grudin, you are *not* enlisting. I don't care what your father says," she huffed loud enough to turn the eyes of Ms. Potts. Sandra raised a hand to indicate she was okay. My heart fell deep inside as a sudden rush of sadness filled me.

"Thomas Grudin?" I asked, and Sandra nodded.

"Tommy?" I asked, and wondered if this was Tommy Grudin, a boy I'd grown up with. The boy who'd been my first kiss?

Sandra raised her brow and said, "My stars, we haven't called him that in years. Up through ninth grade, he was fine with Tommy, but by tenth grade, he insisted we call him Tom. But how did you know?"

Memory bubbles surfaced, including the one I'd pushed down years before. This was Mrs. Grudin sitting across from me, my neighbor from my home town of Fairview, Texas. Was it possible? Could this be the same Mrs. Grudin, who, from time to time, bandaged my skinned knee and treated me to pop-tarts and milk?

"Ma'am, I grew up in Fairview, Texas. I grew up with a Tommy Grudin. My name is Gabby Santiago," I told her. Sandra's eyes opened wide as she reached and touched my face. A large smile blossomed as her cheeks turned red, and she chuckled with a sound of surprise and disbelief.

"Gabby? Gabby Santiago?"

"Yeah. It's me," I answered. My heart warmed, and I could feel a little glow of my own beginning to surface around my neck and on my cheeks. Mrs. Grudin pawed at my face, her smile stretching as she repeated my name a few more times. Memories rifled through my head, and a reservation doused my heart. This was the first person from home I'd had contact with since leaving Fairview. I'd lost my way, and there was a reason for it. I saw Tommy's face in my mind, and the heaviness in my heart took all my thoughts.

"Tommy is dead," I heard myself say, and wished I could have rephrased it.

"He was always so fond of you, Gabby. He really was. And look at you, now. Oh, my girl, such a beautiful young woman you've grown up to become. Oh, and your parents, they must be so happy and so proud," she said, but then stopped, and I could see the questions forming. I knew what was coming. Mr. Grudin came back to the counter to collect his keys and drink down more of his coffee. Mrs. Grudin's manner changed almost immediately. The questions she had were gone. Her face went without expression as she gathered her things. I considered what she'd said earlier: "He won't finish, till he drowns it." I'd wondered what she meant by that, but by now, I think I understood.

As I waved a hand to Mrs. Grudin, she broke her empty expression, and said, "We split our time between here and Fairview, and I see your parents a few times a month. I'll make sure to mention seeing you," she told me, and before I could tell her not to, she was already headed out the door.

6

Philadelphia didn't see its first snow storm until we were well into February. By then, the weather thermometer mounted outside the diner's door struggled to crawl out of the single digits at night. During the day, the feeling of the sun on your face was just a memory as the cold held the thermometer somewhere in the twenties. But on this particular week, the thermometer's silvery finger stretched to reach almost thirty degrees as a new front came up the coastline. Having passed through the Gulf, *it's a Nor'easter*, I heard a few say. At first, I thought I'd heard "North Easter" and even repeated it to a few who were interested in listening. A stout correction was quick and firm. *It's Nor'easter*, I was told, and was sure to phrase it correctly the second, or maybe third, time.

Till now, we'd only seen a couple of small clippers

that delivered a coating of the white stuff. There were also a few storms that spilled rain and caked everything in a thin sheet of ice, but we hadn't seen anything like this. The latest forecast came with its own set of severe winter warnings and advisories. At first, I'd dismissed the warnings as just some news. Soon after, a small flutter of excitement woke in me, and it had an appetite for more. Two feet of snow was expected to fall over a period of just twelve hours: a fast storm with a lot of snow. Now, who doesn't like that?

Growing up in Texas, I saw my share of spring storms. Some were the heaviest you could imagine, with lightning skating across dark skies, and thunder that rattled our windows. We even had a few tornadoes touchdown in our town, and felt the western reach of a hurricane's hand. And once, we survived a flood that carried off one of our cars. But this was my first snow storm. I hated to admit it – I was a storm junkie, and I could hardly contain myself. A smile stayed fixed on my face, and the flutter of excitement grew warmer, keeping my feet moving. As I worked each table and met new faces, the same conversations were just a word or two away.

Did you hear about the weather coming? What's the latest? When is it going to start? I couldn't get enough of it. When new faces sat down, I was sure to work the weather into the conversation. First, I'd take their orders, of course, but then it was my turn. *Heck of a storm coming, did'ya know?* I'd ask, and if they hadn't heard, or wanted to know what the latest forecast was... well, I was more than happy to oblige and spill all that I knew. Sometimes I'd get clever and engage the neighboring booths. A real *provocateur* I was, churning up the excitement like a chef cooking for a king. Necks stretched and turned, elbows and arms cradled the back of the booths, amateur forecasts volleyed back and forth in a burst of heightened speculation. *I heard three feet... well, I heard snow will fall up to four inches an hour.* Delicious. I ate it up. Why wouldn't I? By now, I'd seen some snow, but this was a storm – a massive storm.

There were those who saw the storm as a nuisance, or who thought the forecast was just hyped up news. Admittedly, there were some reservations, but I dismissed their commentary. How dare they spoil my excitement? Of course, I didn't say that aloud. For most of them, like Ms. Potts, I thought they were putting on a front. I told myself that, deep down, they were stifling any excitement and waiting to see what happened. Maybe when there were a few flakes in the air or an inch or two, on the ground to kick your feet through, I'd see the enthusiasm, and they'd join in.

When my tables were all served and I had nobody waiting for me to seat them, Ms. Potts waved an okay for me to take a break. There was no hesitation; I couldn't wait any longer, and grabbed my coat. A snowflake wandered past me as I left the diner. Another followed, and I reached my hand out and plucked it from the air. Standing on the diner's stoop, an older gentlemen walking with a cane offered a polite hello.

"Smells like snow, doesn't it?" he asked in a voice that whistled as he spoke. I wanted to laugh. How can anything smell like snow? But I answered, "Sure – we're gonna have a heck of a good storm, aren't we?" He agreed, and continued on his way. But there was something different in the air, too. It was fresh and damp and very cold, which pinched my chest when I drew in a deep breath. I suppose it did smell like snow. Sure, I'd heard the expression before, but I'd never experienced it.

More snowflakes fell. They were the smaller, fluffy kind that didn't turn or stray. The snow flurries hurried as more appeared around me. White fireflies – the bigger snow flurries – reminded me of the slow wandering of the glowing bugs as I plucked another from the air. The ground was cold, and the snow didn't melt when the flakes landed.

Within a few minutes, I could make out thin white drifts that gathered on the black asphalt and swirled over the street as a cold breeze pick up from behind me. The sight of it was new, and it was beautiful. When I stretched my eyes as far down the street as I could, a wall of snow filled my view. The snow was falling fast, and at a steadier pace. It was happening. The storm was here. Pockets of white stretched and pulled and slithered across the road like a snake racing to catch its prey. Only, the prey was the cars jockeying along the street's curb, looking to park and hibernate during the storm.

Most of the stores were closed, or were in the process of closing. Other than our diner, I expected to find one other place still open: the Irish pub across from us. Both of our places would do well tonight. After all, what a way to celebrate a good storm!

By the time the first orange glow of street lights could be seen through the diner's front window, Philadelphia had over six inches of snow. This was officially the most snow I'd ever seen at any one time. And Angela's, well... we stayed open, and I was the happier for it. Let's face it: we lived just a few blocks away, and our night would have been filled with the same activities – watching the latest forecast on the news, and staring out the window.

A handful of our regulars stayed with us, and I liked having the familiar faces around. There were at least a dozen of them; *a snow party,* I liked to call it. *Keep on Truckin´* was one of mine who'd stopped in for a meal. I could almost always expect to see him on Mondays and Thursdays. He ordered his usual, and kept an eye on the falling snow through the window. He told me he was trying to decide if getting on the road tonight was such a good idea – I didn't think so.

At one point, Clark brought his portable TV to the front and placed it on the counter so that everyone could watch and listen to it. As small as that screen was, I doubt many could see more than a blur of flickering gray light coming from that little white box. But that didn't stop those in the furthest of booths from straining to see the screen.

The TV painted dim white light on the faces of those who'd moved in closer to watch. A few thanked Clark for bringing his portable out to the front, while others gave a nod and a wave in his direction. I saw a smile on Clark's face. It was brief, but I saw it. The different shades of gray light danced a funny jig as the screen went bright and dark. Everyone's eyes widened to eat up the images from the screen of the TV when the forecasted snow totals were shown.

The small figure of a weatherman walked across the screen, pointing to a large map behind him, showing the different areas of Philadelphia. He waved his arms to demonstrate how the storm was moving up the coast and creeping inland. He talked of the expected snowfall amounts, which everyone enjoyed hearing. He told us about the possibility of snow drifts burying parked cars, and said to expect power outages. He even talked about a *food-shopping-meter* to gauge the strength of the storm. Philadelphia was approaching an eight out of ten. Ms. Potts laughed when the weatherman fixed his own cartoon grin next to the animated *food-shopping-meter* on the screen. She let out another giggle before telling everyone that Angela's had more than enough food. It was true, too: Angela's was full of food. At the last check, I did an inventory count, and didn't expect we'd work up a food order for at least another week, maybe two. A crazy thought crossed my mind. What if the drifting snow buried us? What if we were stuck in the diner for days? A week, even?

The collected group in front of the screen sounded a small cheer when our section of the city was mentioned. The cheer grew louder when the weatherman announced that our area was expected to be one of the hardest hit. Butterflies flew and flipped somersaults in my gut, and my heart rose in my chest. More snow. Just for us. I felt giddy. Even Ms. Potts was joining in as I saw her shaking her head with an awed expression playing behind the gray-light reflecting from her glasses. She pushed up on the thick frames and clapped her hands, letting out another giggle when the screen flashed the *food-shopping-meter* on the screen once more.

"Turn that up," *Keep on Truckin'* hollered from his booth. "Gotta know if I'll be heading to Virginia later tonight, or canceling altogether." He held his coffee cup up in the air and gave me a wink. I filled his mug and asked what time he thought he'd need to leave. He wore a thick mustache and a goatee that was at least a year or more grown out. Coffee dripped from his mustache whiskers as he talked about his trip to Sterling, Virginia.

"South of us is getting some snow, too," he said, "but nothing like here in Philly." He went on to tell me that as long as the '95 Corridor stayed open, he could leave by midnight. *Keep on Truckin'* was a solid regular of mine during the last year, a comfortable regular. He was my first regular that I'd adopted from Ms. Potts a few weeks after I'd started. Two, and sometimes three, days a week I'd served him hash and eggs with a side of rye toast. I didn't want to see him on the road. Not tonight.

"You'll be stuck like the rest of 'less you get to leaving before that next foot of snow falls," someone rebutted from the counter. When I went back to offer more coffee, *Keep on Truckin'* had already put his money on the table, and with another wink of his eye, said,

"Think they might be right. Time for me to get on the road. Just need to get to Maryland, and I'll be clear from there." I followed him to the door and wished him a safe drive. I told him Sterling, Virginia would be there tomorrow if he needed to pull over and sleep the storm out. He gave me a peculiar smile.

"Thanks, Mother, I'll do that," he laughed, and

squeezed his face until I heard the sound of a lip-puckered kiss come from beneath his mustache.

"Just be safe," I added and jokingly wagged a finger in his direction as he left the diner.

When I peered through the door to watch *Keep on Truckin'* navigate the snow on foot, it occurred to me just how bad this much snow could be. The street lights, as far into the distance as I could see, told the story of how fast the snow was falling. Looking into their radiant dome shapes, washes of heavy snow pelted down on the streets at an incredible pace. It wasn't like the flurries that seemed to float and go nowhere. It was practically raining snow. The thought of being here all night, or a couple of days, crossed my mind again. Certainly the morning shift wouldn't be digging themselves out in time to prep for the rush in the morning. And then I laughed... what rush? Nobody would be digging out of this snow for at least another day.

A dark figure of a man appeared in the snow. He approached the diner from the middle of the street. There were no plows, no cars. In fact, there was nothing at all. The black asphalt and parked cars and small lawns in front of the shops were all gone. Nothing was outside except a snow desert reflecting the orange-yellow glow of Philadelphia street lights. The desert was barren – empty, except for the figure of this one man.

When the figure walked into the light of a street

lamp, I could see a heavy trench coat hung over his broad shoulders, and a gentleman's hat, the kind I'd seen at church when I was younger. A fedora, I think it was called. Only, his was pitched down to hide his face. When he was almost directly under the street lamp, a halo of orange light encircled him. The snow reached half the distance to his knees. While the figure of the man was easy enough to see, his face remained a secret, hidden behind a shadow cast by the brim of his hat.

When his upturned face spied the diner, with me standing in the stoop, he stabbed at the air with a clumsy wave, and pushed forward through the near knee-high snow. I was content with the company we already had, minus *Keep on Truckin´*. I knew all the faces, and most of their names. If we were going to ride out this storm, drinking hot chocolate and watching Clark's portable TV, then, selfishly, I was happy not to add any more.

As the man in the trench coat entered, he didn't look up, or say hello. Instead, he made his way to an empty booth in the corner, and took a seat, coat and hat still on. It was Ms. Potts' station, and she was already standing and picking a menu up from the counter.

More gray lights played back on the faces of the folks huddled around Clark's TV. The weatherman was back at the map of Philadelphia, his arms motioning up and down and pointing out snow totals.

"Any change?" I asked, but knew that, even if the rest of the storm were suddenly cancelled, I'd still be happy with the amount of snow sitting outside.

"Nope – still calling for the same," a voice began to say. And, after a short pause, they continued, "But there is a chance the storm will slow, and, if it does, then we could see up to thirty-two inches. Can you imagine? That's almost three feet of snow," they finished, excitement heightened to a near shrill.

Three feet, or almost three feet! I pitched my hand up against my thigh, trying to imagine just how much snow that would be. Without warning, the crash of a coffee pot against the floor exploded in a sound of spilling and tumbling glass. All the eyes in the diner found Ms. Potts. The man in the dark fedora was seated, his back against the wall, facing everyone. When the last piece of glass stopped bouncing, the weatherman's voice was the only sound we heard. Ms. Potts stepped back from the corner booth. A piece of glass crunched beneath her shoe as she put a hand over her mouth.

"What you want?" she barked at him, "You ain't said enough before? You ain't got enough answers?" she began to push some of the glass on the floor with the tip of her shoe. Clark walked past me, a dustpan and broom in his hands. When he knelt to clean up the broken coffee pot, the man in the corner eased his hat off and placed it on the table. Clark stopped cleaning; he didn't move.

"And who's this?" the man asked as he tilted his chin in my direction. "She's new here – and cute, too. Very cute. Haven't seen her before. Of course, it's only been a few years, hasn't it, Ms. Potts? And how are we doing, Clark?" he finished in a rusty voice that sounded crippled from years of smoking. The diner stayed silent. Ms. Potts remained standing, while Clark singled out a larger piece of glass and picked it up. Clark's eyes stayed on the man in the corner.

"Can I help you?" I blurted out, and then wished I hadn't. Ms. Potts shook her head in a quiet scolding, and I knew that meant she wanted me to remain unheard. Stay, but say nothing.

"Ahhh," the man coughed out, "chipper, aren't you? And what is your name, deary?" he asked, leaning forward and placing his hands on the table. Nerves settled in, dousing the warm lift of excitement from the snow storm. Maybe it was the look on Ms. Potts' face, or the way Clark took care in clearing the broken glass from the floor, slow and cautious. But what I think made me afraid more than anything, was seeing how my friends feared the man with the fedora.

He was an older man with nothing spectacular about him: he had white thinning hair combed straight back, with a receding widow's peak above his forehead. The skin below the peak was deeply creased with thick lines that rested atop heavy eyebrows, which went wild in the corners. Deep cuts traveled away from his eyes, and moved down his cheeks to his jaw. I thought maybe there was a time he had dimples that girls liked, thinking they were cute, but they had been gone for some time.

As he picked up his hat and followed the brim of it with his fingers, I noticed large age spots on his hands. Some were browning, and others stood out almost as white as the snow outside. Dropping of glass pulled my eyes as I turned to Clark, who continued cleaning the floor. Clark kept his sights on the man. There was something else in the diner with us. I couldn't see it or smell it like the snow before the storm began, but I could tell that it was tension and worry.

"Well?" the man growled sharply, and I jumped where I stood. "What is it?"

"What is what?" I asked, and thought my voice sounded tiny and child-like.

"Your name, deary? You see, I know Ms. Potts, here, and I know Clark. Heck, we've all known each other near twenty years. But, deary, I don't know you, and I don't know your name." Twenty years, the man said. Twenty years. The scolding in Ms. Potts' eyes had faded, as did her strong posture. She now stood with her shoulders slumped. This wasn't my Ms. Potts. This wasn't my Clark. This was a family that was alien and foreign to me. It scared me.

"I'm Gabby, sir. And can I fix you a cup of coffee, or get you a bite to eat?" As I finished offering one of my better *waitressy* deliveries, the man slapped the table and let out a boisterous laugh that ended in choked coughs. He cupped a hand over his mouth and hollowed out a year or more of sediment that had settled deep inside his lungs. Surely, I considered, this old broken man couldn't be a threat to Ms. Potts, or Clark? The tension remained, but the edges were gripped by confusion. When his coughing fit was over, he let out one last guffaw, and pulled an envelope from inside his trench coat.

"Well, Miss Gabby, my name is Detective Ramiz. I'm one of Philadelphia's finest – have been most of my adult life," he began to say and, moved his eyes to stare at the envelope in his hands. His words went softer, as he continued, "That is nearly forty-years of my life. One job. One purpose," he finished.

Ms. Potts motioned her eyes to me, and then to the coffee makers. The diner was silent again, with only the weatherman's voice to fill the dead air. Nobody lifted a fork or spoon. Instead, they watched and listened as I approached the table. Turning over the mug in front of the detective, I poured for him a fresh cup of coffee. He gave me a smile, and I thought his eyes seemed warmer, more pleasant, now that I was closer to him.

"I'm glad we can be civil, Ms. Potts," he exclaimed,

lifted his cup, and motioned a gesture in her direction. He drank it black, no sugar, no cream, just black.

"What is it you want? Our business was over twenty years ago, and then fifteen years ago, and then again ten years ago," Ms. Potts addressed him with a tone I'd heard only once or twice before when chasing out undesirables.

The detective held up the envelope in his hand. He waved it back and forth, and let out a forced sigh.

"You see this, here – these are my walking papers. Forced retirement. Full bennies and pension, and all that comes with getting old. I'm *out,* and..." he stopped and dropped his hand with the envelope on the table. Whatever the reason for the retirement, it wasn't his decision. The detective took a sip of his coffee. When he was ready, he faced Ms. Potts.

"Almost two-hundred cases have come across my desk in my career. Do you know how many are left open?" he asked, then turned to Clark, and then to me, and back to Ms. Potts. "I know *you* know. Don't you, Ms. Potts? How about you, Clark, I know *you* know, too. Why don't you both tell Miss Gabby, here, how many cases I might be leaving open before they cart me off to rot in a retirement community, or old-folks home, or *wherever* it is they push out old dogs to die?" Ms. Potts and Clark passed words with their eyes, and then I saw Ms. Potts mouth the word 'one'.

"What was that? Say it. I want to hear you say it!"

the detective said, raising his voice.

"One, sir. It is one case," Ms. Potts answered, her voice breathy and weak.

"YES, it is. One in my entire career, I've solved all but one case!" he bellowed loudly, as though preaching to a room of followers. "Well, how about that? But maybe I'm not done. Maybe Philadelphia's finest is going to get a shock when I come in with my final *one* case solved!" he chortled, and then coughed up more sediment. He pulled in a mouthful of coffee and forced it down.

"Can't you just let it go?" Ms. Potts began to ask, "Can't you please let this thing go?" The detective dropped his coffee cup to the table, and grabbed his fedora. As he stood in front of me, he put himself back together with a practiced efficiency. Within seconds, the dark figure I'd first glimpsed under the street light was standing in front of us. He lifted his head to reveal his face, and answered.

"Because, Ms. Potts, you and Clark, your ex-con, there, are guilty of killing a man. Guilty of a murder. I know it in my heart. And you know it, too. I aim to finish this," he said evenly, and made his way to the door. *Murder? Ms. Potts and Clark? Ex-con? Who have I been working with for the last year?* This had to be a mistake. There was no way!

When the bell above the door rang, tension spilled out of the diner like the snow falling to the ground, only to be replaced by a mountain of questions. But the detective didn't leave, not at first, anyway. He closed the door briefly, and turned back to face us again.

"By the way, word on the street is that Angela's Diner is for sale. There's also word that there might be an interested buyer; very interested. And they have no plans on keeping your little diner – they'll be tearing it down. And we all know what that means," he finished. Then he opened the door to leave. Snow flew in high above him, and low around him. It spiraled in the air with a momentum carried by the winter wind pushing inside. When the door closed, the hovering snow fell to the floor, settling on Clark, who was shaking his head, and clearing the broken glass.

Ms. Potts approached the booth where the detective had sat. Her steps were slow, and seemed crippled. When she reached the booth, she clutched the table, and held herself up. She pushed on her glasses and gulped for air. She gave a worried look first to Clark, and then to me. I wanted to run to her. I wanted to take her hands and help her sit. I wanted to tell her it would be okay. But I didn't. I didn't do anything.

Later, when I'd finally rested my head on my pillow, I dreamed about the snow storm. But it wasn't a happy dream. It wasn't filled with the same excitement I'd felt earlier. Instead, I saw the deserted street in front of Angela's Diner. A blinding rush of falling snow covered the cars and the lawns and the buildings. I saw the figure of a dark man wearing a fedora, standing directly under a street light. An orange-yellow glow surrounded him as he laughed a hideous sound. Ms. Potts' body lay at his feet, motionless. A spread of blood grew and reddened the snow around her while the detective's heinous laughter echoed like the rolling of distant thunder.

7

A few weeks had gone by since experiencing my first actual snow storm. More than thirty inches of the white stuff was dumped on us. We took turns unburying the stoop and the sidewalk in front of the diner. A few of our regular customers even joined in and helped shovel during the storm, keeping our walkway clear by removing a few inches at a time. The snow was fluffier than I expected. It was feather-light, and didn't pack together at all like some of the snow we had earlier in the year. I tried to make a snowball. I even tried to throw one in the street, only to see a confetti bomb of loose flurries explode from my closed hand.

The snow was so light that I played magic tricks with it. Waving my hand over the top of the snow, I could pull up a handful of flurries and have them chase my fingers before falling again. Someone mentioned it was a cold and dry snow, with very little moisture, so it stayed extra fluffy. It sounded funny, like something you'd order at a bakery. What I liked most was that shoveling wasn't much of a chore, although I can't say the rest of the city agrees. After all, thirty-plus inches of anything is bound to slow things a little. Or a lot.

In all, the storm shut down most of the greater Philadelphia area. Cars were buried – first by the drifting snow, and then after the streets were plowed. Busses, trains, and airplane flights were all cancelled. The winds that pushed the snow up into drifts also brought down phone lines and some power lines. At least five deaths were directly attributed to the storm. Two of those were an elderly husband and wife only three blocks from my apartment. Their house filled with a poisonous gas when a vent on their roof became blocked by snow and ice. The news reported that they went to sleep that evening, and never woke up.

Angela's Diner was one of the few places that stayed open. We lost our phone lines for a day or so, but we never lost power. Clark said the grill ran on gas, anyway. He said he'd cook up whatever was in the fridge, and then leave it outside. I thought that was clever. According to the thermometer, temperatures were still hovering around twenty, which was already colder than any refrigerator we had.

The Irish Pub across from us stayed open, too. I'd

seen a few comings and goings as I passed by in a walk to the diner from my apartment. And, as usual, some of their regulars were swaying, and some were falling, and most had overstayed their welcome. Fortunately for us, those stumbling had made their way home to their own beds, and didn't stop in for a bite at the diner. A part of me was happy to see that the fast-food restaurant was shut-down by the storm. And it wasn't just closed during the snowfall, it remained closed for the better part of three days. Angela's saw more new faces during those three days than we'd seen in the previous two weeks.

One of the faces I'd not seen back at the diner was the detective's; not that I'd care to see his face, anyway. He'd come in to bid his warnings to Ms. Potts and Clark, and then left. He said one case, just a single case of his remained open and unsolved. Days passed, and I wondered how it could be that the detective's single case involved two of the most caring and loving people I'd ever come to know.

A few times, I caught myself wanting to ask about Detective Ramiz. I was a breath away, once – I'd had my hand up with a question on my tongue, as though I were back in grade school. Ms. Potts walked from the back and stopped where she stood. She fixed me a look as if ready to answer a question she hadn't heard yet. She was like that – she could read me, especially when there was something on my mind. But I didn't ask. I'm not sure if it was because I didn't want to think any differently about my new family, or because I knew that, if I opened the book on their past, then maybe I'd obligate myself to opening the book on my own. I wasn't ready to do that. I don't know if I'll ever be ready. I shrugged away the pending questions, and Ms. Potts lifted her chin in a quick nod before continuing on with her work.

By the time some measure of normalcy had become more a part of our every day, the snows had receded like the flood waters I remember seeing as a kid. Gone were the large drifts that swallowed the smaller cars. Gone were the lawn chairs from the streets and curb that folks used to claim a parking spot as their own. Some interesting fights grew out of that practice.

What were left were street-length rolls of blackened snow hugging the curbs, along with mountains of plowed storm remains in the supermarket parking lots. The only white snow that could be seen anywhere was the square patches of lawn that sat in front of row-homes and a few businesses. Angela's Diner didn't have a lawn to call its own, so I adopted the one in the front of my apartment: Ms. Potts' house. But that, too, began to shrink as the weather warmed. And, by the time we entered into March, the edges of the snow melted to reveal the grasses that lay sleeping, waiting for spring to arrive. By then, I was itching for spring, too. I think we all were.

I jumped when I heard the shattering of glass on the

diner's floor. The tumbling pieces of reminded me of the coffee pot and Detective Ramiz. Thoughts of pending spring weather disappeared as images of a dark figure in a fedora entered my mind. I could see Clark kneeling, and Ms. Potts standing at the booth, their expressions tortured and afraid.

"Sorry about that, Gabby," I heard, and saw Jarod Patreu, an 'oops' expression on his face, and an empty light bulb box in his hand.

"Shame, it was new, too," I answered back, smiling.

"Slipped right out of the box. Last one, of course. Gonna have to go pick up more on my run to the hardware store."

"Jarod Patreu – what'd ya do now?" Ms. Potts exclaimed from behind me. "We pay you to fix what we can't fix. We ain't paying you to break things, too," she complained, but I could hear the playfulness in her voice. She was fond of Jarod, and was having fun with him.

"I'm sorry, Ms. Potts. Bulb slipped, just slipped right out of the box. I'll replace it," he answered, his voice sounded disappointed. I started to feel bad for him: Ms. Potts was teasing, and he had no idea.

Ms. Potts walked around front with the broom in one hand, and passed me the dust pan. She was smiling by now, and said, "Baby, you ain't gotta buy nothing. Heck, Gabby, here, dropped more dishes her first month than you done broke anything in all the years you been helping."

"How did I get dragged into this?" I jokingly complained, but knew I was only playing a supporting role in the conversation.

Shallow relief settled on Jarod's face as he stepped down off the chair. "You must have broke a lot of things, huh?" he said, smiling, and then added, "thank you, Ms. Potts. I've got to pick up a few more things tonight, anyway."

When we finished cleaning up the broken bulb, Jarod gathered some loose tools he'd brought out, and tucked them away in the yellowing tool bag he wore around his waist. Watching him, I had a memory of home and my parent's garage. A workbench lined the far wall, black drawers, and a wood top. A back board stood behind the bench with pegs sticking out to hang tools on. Growing up, I learned how to fix things; a lot of things. That sounds odd for a girl, but I enjoyed it. And I was good at it.

"You carry a lot of tools with you. Heavy?" I asked, as Jarod tucked a screwdriver away. He gave me a half-smile, then shuffled his feet before answering,

"Yeah, a little. Need to have a variety, and all – time to time, stores need something different... that is, I've gotta lot of places to manage," he answered in a shy voice with sweet eyes. Until now, I hadn't really noticed his eyes. But, standing closer to him and talking a little about nothing at all, I realized I liked his eyes.

Taller than me and a few years older, Jarod was the diner's handyman. With unkempt brown hair that hung over his ears, and stray locks that fell in front of his eyes, I liked the messiness of his hair. Ms. Potts liked his hair, too – she'd poke fun some nights after he'd left the diner, motioning a whoosh of her hand to mimic him throwing back his thick bangs from in front of his eyes. While she might have liked his hair, she loved his dimples. Don't you just wanna pinch 'em cheeks, eat 'em up? she'd squeal, and clap her hands, laughing.

Jarod showed up once a week. You could set your clock by him. He was never late, never missed a date. He always came once a week on Thursdays. He'd spend the afternoon fixing whatever needed fixing, and, when our list of to-do work was short, or when we had no list at all, which sometimes happened, he'd fall back on a list of his own. He called it his preventative maintenance list, and, with it, he'd work from corner to corner, and front to back. Angela's Diner was just one of a dozen of his regular customers. He tended to all the stores on Park Street, and even a few on neighboring avenues.

"Gotta run to the hardware store," he began, and lifted the empty light bulb box, "So, umm, I'll see you when I get back?" he finished, raising his brow, as though asking.

"Well, duh," I joked, and flipped up my waist apron.

"I work here. Tell you what, when you get back. I'll fix you a late lunch, early dinner. A man's gotta eat, right?"

Jarod's eyes grew, and his dimples appeared on his cheeks out of nowhere, like a magic trick, "Sure – I'd like that." I offered a warm expression; not *waitressy*, but instead, just me. Walking him to the door, I couldn't help but wonder if he liked my eyes too. When he was gone, Ms. Potts was waiting like a cat, ready to pounce on its prey.

"Mmmm-hmmm, you're gonna fix my Jarod something? Girl, you like that boy, don't you? You do, don't you?" she said, letting out a small laugh. At first I thought she was joking. But then I considered my offer to fix him a meal, and thought of his eyes. Confused feelings stirred in me. I mean, I liked Jarod, but he was Jarod. Did I like him in that way? Years, I heard in my head. Not weeks, or months, but years. I hadn't looked at anyone, or considered anyone, in years.

"Uhhh, no. Don't get me wrong, Jarod is cute, but I was only being polite," I answered cautiously. But hearing the sound of my voice, I wondered if Ms. Potts knew I was lying.

"Gabby, you know that boy likes you. As far I can see, he's liked you the better half of the year. Didn't you see the red warming up his cheeks when you was talking to him? So, you got nothing for him?" she asked, sounding disappointed. Heat crept up on my neck, and embarrassment settled deep inside. Grabbing a towel, I took to the counter, and wiped what didn't need wiping. Ms. Potts joined in, and also wiped what didn't need wiping. An unexpected rush of emotion squeezed my insides. I felt awkward and uncomfortable, and tried to keep my eyes to the counter in front of me.

Finally, I mumbled, "I haven't looked at a boy like that in a long time." And, suddenly, I felt terribly sad and unimportant. I stopped wiping the counter. I had to. Ms. Potts came around the counter to face me.

"Girl, it's okay. Just thought you keeping company with someone your own age might be a good thing. Might be good for you," she answered, and then added, "The boy does like you, though," she finished with a whispered cheer to my ear. My heart thumped, and a warm feeling followed. The thought of a boy liking me wasn't unknown or alien, it was just something I'd forgotten about until now. Ms. Potts nudged my arm. She nudged it again and again until I broke a smile and nudged her arm back. "Jarod got eyes for you, Gabby-girl... Jarod got eyes..." she sang to me with soft words.

"Do you think so?" I said, delighted. "Really?" I wondered if it was so, and then giggled at the thought, and at the song. We spent the next fifteen minutes talking about boys. Talking like two teenage girls would talk. And we even talked a little more about Jarod, and his dimples, and that hair. Before I knew it, I felt somewhat comfortable – maybe even a little normal.

8

It was my turn to work the newspaper's crossword puzzle. Mondays are a slow day at Angela's. They have been every week that I've worked at the diner. Just why that is... well, that's anyone's guess. As for the crossword, I penciled in a word, and then a second and third. And then, I found the first word was wrong. Annoyance gripped my hand when I found the pencil's eraser had been chewed off. Gross. I'm partial to word-searches and pencil-mazes, anyway.

The tick and clack of a bug bumping against the front window pulled my eyes. A blur of black and iridescence bumped the glass a few more times before deciding to move on. It was the first bug of the spring season, and it was a big one. I kept to my seat. Most of the Philadelphia winter had melted away. My first major snow storm was just a fading memory. And, like most, I was looking forward to seeing little green spring buds on the trees, and dandelions interrupt the emerging patches of grass.

By now, the snow was gone from the lawns, and the grass was already starting to come alive with brighter colors that seemed to glow in the orange light of the setting sun. A few plowed mounds of winter snow remained in the supermarket parking lots. Eclipsed with black soot from the pollution of passing cars and trucks, they were more an eyesore than playful snowy reminders. But these, too, were shrinking, and I think the entire Philadelphia area was happy with that.

The mercury in the thermometer outside our door was stretching its silvery finger for the top lines. The silver reached past more lines from day to day. And folks passing by the diner were beginning to wear less. One day, the wool hats and thick scarves were gone. Soon after that, the gloves and mittens were off their hands, and their heavier winter coats were put away for the year. Even the teenagers passing the diner were donning lighter jackets. Teenagers and business-types, and an occasional elderly couple passed by Angela's Diner with the same smiles and focused eyes eating up the warming sunlight. Springtime was on the way.

I saw Mr. Thurmon's car pull up in front of the diner. He pushed his arms around the steering wheel, and parallel parked in one move. It was impressive and swift. Down in Texas, Mr. Thurmon wouldn't have to parallel park. *There is more of everything, and everything is bigger.* I snickered at the thought, and wished to share the joke, but I was working alone this afternoon. Ms. Potts had a doctor's appointment, and scheduled it weeks ago; we all scheduled appointments and such on Mondays, when the diner was at its slowest. There was Clark and me, and, for the most part, empty booths, counters, and lonely stool tops.

Mr. Thurmon was slow to get out of his car. I watched as he struggled to open the car door. He heaved a push until it was open, and, when he was ready, he swung his legs out and firmed his grip to help pull himself up. When he was standing, his face cramped and swelled to a red shine. He was trying to push the pain away. It was his arthritis. From the history Ms. Potts shared, Mr. Thurmon was following a course that ultimately took his mother.

As the pain passed, an odd expression remained on his face. It wasn't success, or the triumph of standing, or even pride from having accomplished something. It was sorrow and vulnerability. And I think I understood what he might be feeling – it made me sad when I considered it. From this point forward, every day, *that* day, was going to be his best day for the rest of his life. Today, as he struggled with living with the pain in his body, today was going to be as good as he was ever going to feel.

Today was his *best* day. Tomorrow, it would get worse, and the day after that, even worse. I jumped when a rush of wind blew up behind Mr. Thurmon as a truck passed within a few inches of hitting him. He jumped, too, and the rush of the truck cleared his expression to one of awe and shock. Today might have been the best day of the rest of his life, but it was also close to being his last.

While the diner was home to Clark, Ms. Potts, and me, I didn't want to see it sold. I understood why Mr. Thurmon would want to let it go, though. I don't think any of us would have done differently. When Mr. Thurmon saw me through the window, he waved and pushed a smile onto his face. The crossword would wait; I was happy to get the door for him. Lasting for just a moment, the sound of cars and people and birds invaded the quiet of the diner. The smell of spring followed Mr. Thurmon, as the bell echoed above our heads. Almost on cue, Clark popped out from the back, and took to his station behind the grill.

"Afternoon, M-Mr. Thurmon," Clark said, and motioned a wave with his spatula, as if saluting.

"How goes it, there, Clark? Cooking up a storm?" Mr. Thurmon asked, his voice fading, as he glanced around to the empty corners of the diner, and then back to the clean counters. He looked in my direction, his face a bit pinched with disappointment. "Anything today? Anything at all?"

"I saw a few tickets come in this morning, but nothing since Clark and I have been on," I answered with a shrug of my shoulders. I hated having to tell him we opened this afternoon empty, and had stayed empty since.

As he walked around the counter to the cash register, there was a slow drag in his step; a stutter. Had it been there before, or had it just developed? I could see the tip of his right shoe catching some of the floor. Mr. Thurmon wore his lawyerly best, and looked handsome. I could imagine him twenty years younger – very handsome, indeed. His shoes, especially the right, bore scuff marks from the shoe tips and across the faces. Just how long has he had the arthritis? Maybe he felt something was wrong with him, but was quick to dismiss it. Maybe he pushed off any visits to the doctor's office in favor of working. Or maybe he knew all along what was wrong, and that there was little to be done about it. He intentionally pushed the inevitable.

From the cash register, he gave an apologetic look, as if it were his fault the diner remained empty. As he stood there, arranging the register's drawer, he flinched and pulled his hand up. He made a fist, then shook his fingers down at the ground. The same cramped expression showed briefly on his face before passing. My heart gushed, and I wanted to hug him and tell him how sorry I was that this was happening to him. I didn't know his mother, but I did know him, and he was one of our family, too. I thought of him as our goofy uncle, the one who visits unexpectedly, and gets everyone riled up and laughing before disappearing until his next visit.

"Well, I suppose I shouldn't expect much different on a Monday. The day has never been a particularly good day," he explained in a matter-of-fact way, and then asked, "Gabby, you alright?" The question was a surprise, and I wondered if I was just staring. I sometimes did that, not on purpose.

"Oh, yes, I'm sorry, Mr. Thurmon. I'm fine, just a little tired, is all. Been cleaning, you know, *time to lean, time to clean*," I answered back, and offered a grin that I hoped didn't look as goofy as it sounded.

"Okay, then. No need to tire yourself," he began, and gave the diner a once over with his eyes, "Does look good and clean enough to eat off of."

"C-Can I fix you something, a q-quick meal?" Clark offered from behind the grill.

Mr. Thurmon paused, as if considering when he last ate, and looked at his watch to maybe confirm it.

"Ya know, Clark, yes. I think I'll do just that. Thank you. How about a grilled cheese and some fries? And I'll get my own coffee. And, Gabby, you have a customer," he finished, and motioned to the door.

What I saw next was like something that had walked clear off the front of a magazine cover. A beautiful woman entered our little diner, wearing an emerald green evening gown. A glamorous figure with white skin and red hair draping around her shoulders with piercing green eyes that matched her gown, the woman looked stunning. I had to admit to being glad it was any day other than Thursday, and that Jarod was somewhere else – anywhere else.

Insecurity tugged at me, and I pulled my hands around my collar and waist apron, and tried to tidy my outfit. Next, my hands were in my hair, pushing back what might've strayed. I felt uncomfortable and frumpy standing in the same room with someone so lovely and radiant. It was a struggle to stay where I was. I wanted to go to the back, but Ms. Potts wasn't here. Shuffling my feet, I watched and waited for the magazine cover in front of me to realize she'd entered the wrong building.

The woman seemed to float across the floor, her green dress hovering just above her feet, as glimpses of expensive heels peeked from beneath. A pearl necklace hung around the nape of her neck, their colors and sheen reminding me of the early spring clouds pushing out the winter. A foot in high heels appeared briefly through the dress' slit, her shoes gave her a few inches of height, and were adorned in tiny gemstones, which reflected all the light in the diner.

Mr. Thurmon and Clark were both stopped, and standing in fixed poses – their eyes wide, mouths open.

At some point, I began to wonder what in the world a magazine cover was doing in Angela's Diner. But then the magazine cover was approaching me. She was looking at me. Lips the same shade of red as her hair filled my view, as the woman leaned in and kissed my cheek. Smells of herbal shampoos, and perfume, and expensive bath soaps filled my nose. She smelled as beautiful as she looked. And I thought I must smell as frumpy as I looked.

"You believe this looker, here? A real stunner. Mmmm!" I heard a shout from behind the magazine cover. It was Ms. Potts' voice. Stepping back from the woman, I peered around the emerald green evening gown to find Ms. Potts standing behind her. Shaking her head, she eyed the magazine cover up and down, and repeated, "A real stunner, Suzette. You cleaned up good. Real good!" It was Suzette, and, yes, as Ms. Potts stated, she cleaned up good, real good.

"Gabby, do I look *that* different? I mean, I've got some make-up on, and had my hair done. I wanted to stop in and see you guys," Suzette's voice sang out in a surprise. And, as I looked at my friend, I found my eyes wandering to study different places. You know the ones. The place where there was a deep cut on her lip. And the place above her cheek that swelled and had blackened her eye. But they were clear. In fact, there was nothing there at all. Even the flower-petal bruises on her arm had disappeared. Like the winter storm, they were just a memory.

I'd seen enough by now to know that the bruises and the cuts healed, but the damage done was deeper. It was rooted in a place that make-up and heels and a nice dress couldn't cover up. Suzette was my friend, though, and I was happy that she was happy. She was beautiful; a stunner, as Ms. Potts said a few more times.

"Oh my gosh, Suzette, you look amazing! We almost didn't recognize you walking in here and looking like that. Did we?" I complimented, and turned to Clark and Mr. Thurmon. They continued to stand statuesque, their mouths agape, and shaking an agreeable *no* to my question. I looked for the drool to slip from their mouths, but it didn't.

"Okay, boys, you can close your yaps, now."

Mr. Thurmon blinked a comical flurry of his eyes, and giggled. "You look very beautiful. Special occasion?" he asked.

"We're going to a dinner party – a celebration. And then later, I have some news. It's a surprise for him," she gleamed. "He is going to be so happy!"

Suzette twirled around for the men, smiling with an elegance that was so very fitting for her. There was a glow and confidence that made me happy to see it. She deserved a night to be a queen, a night to be waited and doted on. I was happy for her. We all were.

Suzette was back in the diner later that evening. I'd hoped I wouldn't see her again. Not tonight, anyway. I think we all hoped we wouldn't see her again. I'd hoped that the night she told us about would be hers. A fresh memory, a good memory. A memory that she could draw on when she needed to smile. That is what I had hoped for her. But that wasn't what happened.

When Suzette entered the diner that evening, her hair was a twisted mess. Some of it had been pulled and ripped out. Just above her left ear, a large patch of her hair was missing. The color of her scalp stood out bright against the red of her hair, and was covered with dots of blood that had bubbled and dried. She repeatedly tried to cover her exposed head with some of her longer hair, but, after a minute, it would fall back into place.

The cloudy pearls that draped across her neckline were gone. The elegance and beauty of Suzette's dress was lost. The ripped and torn green fabric from below her neck line hinted to us the dress' secrets of what had happened. From the top of her shoulder and down her left arm, a long patch of her skin was scraped away. Some of her skin remained torn open and bleeding. Blood traveled down, and dripped from her elbow, leaving crimson spots around her feet. It was a huge rash of scratches. Tiny stones sat embedded in her skin, with blood pushing around them. Some of the torn skin was beginning to weep a clear wetness, and scab over.

Suzette wasn't crying, or telling us that it was her fault. Suzette didn't say much of anything, at all. I think it was the silence that scared me. We'd seen her beaten before, far worse than this, in fact. But always, she talked to us, and let us talk to her. Her hand trembled, and her fingers felt like ice. It was cold outside, and she had nothing on but her ruined evening gown. I wondered how far she'd walked. She was just a pale version of the beautiful magazine cover that'd earlier come in to say hello. Her lips were a gray shade of blue, and it was then that I noticed how pale she actually was. While her skin was fair, Suzette looked pallid, almost ashen, with an empty stare in her eyes.

"Suzette, girl... can you tell us what happened to you?" Ms. Potts asked in a concerned voice. With a small towel and clean water, I started to wash the blood and what I thought might be road gravel from her shoulder.

"Suzette, are you hurt anywhere else?" Ms. Potts asked again, sounding like one of those shows on television with the emergency room doctors asking twenty questions. "Girl's hurtin´ the way no woman should hurt," Ms. Potts mumbled as she worked her way around Suzette.

When Suzette lifted her chin to look at us, a broken, thin voice escaped her lips, "I think my baby is dead," was all she said, and then moved her eyes in a blank stare to the floor,

Both Ms. Potts and I looked down. We didn't see anything, except the blood from her arm. When Ms. Potts pulled up on Suzette's emerald green dress, we saw that Suzette was standing in a tiny puddle of blood. Thin lines of bright red cut through the white of her long legs. A new line of blood ran from the insides of her thigh, and then covered the gemstones of her right shoe. Another line formed, and ran past my fingers. It covered the top of her other shoe, washing out more of the gemstones with her blood. We wasted no time. I yelled to Clark to call for an ambulance. Suzette saw the blood, too, and began to tremble all over. From her head to legs, she shook, and grabbed at her middle.

"Girl's in shock," Ms. Potts said as we took hold of Suzette's arms, expecting her to faint. But she didn't.

"My baby," she murmured, and then began to scream. She continued to scream until the ambulance arrived. By then, Suzette lost any of the remaining strength she'd used to get to Angela's Diner, and collapsed.

A day later, we learned through some of our regulars that the official report from the hospital named a Suzette Wilkerson as having sustained injury after falling down a set of steps. Of her injuries, none were life-threatening. In addition, Suzette Wilkerson suffered a miscarriage; she was three months pregnant.

Ms. Potts and I looked at each other, and considered what the report said. Could she have fallen? Certainly a fall down some steps could cause a miscarriage. But, if she had fallen, then why did she come to the diner? Why didn't her husband rush her to the hospital? And her hair, what had happened to her hair? The debate lasted just a minute. We looked at each other. Although we didn't know exactly (we'd learn that later), we knew her injuries were by the hand of her husband.

We didn't see Suzette again for almost a month. By then, she was well enough to stop in for coffee. A few injuries remained, some puffiness and scratches and bruises, but nothing we weren't already familiar with. She pulled and pinned her hair over to one side in way that anyone who didn't see her that night wouldn't know that she was hiding a shallow patch of new hair trying to grow in. All of us greeted her at the door. Even Clark came around front and gave her a peck on the cheek, and a big hug. The three of us stood there with Suzette, and we circled around the same comments about leaving him that had been said a hundred times before. Suzette started nodding her head. She nodded, and then said *I know, I know,* at least a half dozen times. As we continued to spout more of the same, she finally hollered a stern *I know,* and then followed it with a quick smile. She was ready.

Unlike other times, she didn't defend her husband.

She didn't stick up for him, or justify what he'd done. If anything, she sounded cold, maybe callous. She was different. It was easy to understand why. Who wouldn't understand that? She was different because the life she was carrying inside her for more than three months was gone. A new kind of pain was in her eyes. It was loss. She made a decision that night. She was ready.

It was a fairy-tale evening. We were witnesses to the start of it, and to the end of it. Suzette and husband were the handsome couple at the party. It was a high-society invitation-only gathering of some of Philadelphia's most influential people. Suzette's husband, Jim, had been made partner at his law firm earlier that week. This was a celebration for him.

The celebration with her husband felt fresh and new, like it had when they first met. Jim was a gentleman, attentive, touchy, and loving. He wanted to dance with his wife, and he told her how much he loved to hold her. The evening took Suzette back to when the two of them were first falling in love; when it was simple and easy, and when a kiss from him carried her heart for the evening, and sometimes into the next day. He showed a side of him that she remembered falling in love with. They were twenty stories up in the sky, looking out across the Philadelphia skyline, when he held her and told her he loved her. She wanted to get him home and into bed to make love to him all night, the way they used to.

Driving home, she'd saved the biggest news of the evening for her husband. She waited until they were alone, when it could be more intimate, and so that they could remember the moment for the rest of their lives. They were driving down Frankford Avenue, and had just crossed over Pennypack Park. Suzette unbuckled her seat belt, leaned over the car's center console, and whispered in his ear that she loved him. When he smiled, she leaned in closer, and pressed her lips against him with a kiss. She whispered that he was going to be a father. His smile disappeared. His expression went flat, and then his face erupted. He shoved the car's brake pedal to the floor, throwing Suzette into the dashboard, and the windshield, which spidered a web of cracks that stretched and bulged.

Dazed, Suzette pushed and pulled her body down, and fell back into the passenger seat. Her ears were ringing, and her vision blurred. She could make out her husband's voice, and his screaming amidst the low hum stinging inside her head. He was screaming that she'd done this on purpose, that she'd gotten pregnant just when she knew he'd been made partner. But, of course, none of this was true. Suzette couldn't have known about his promotion – not three months ago.

"When he took hold of my hair, and pulled, I knew."

"Knew what?" Ms. Potts asked.

"I knew it was over. I knew that I had to leave him. He pulled my head down, and punched, and kicked me!" she hollered, as tears filled her eyes and ran down her face. "I mean, who does that? Who punches their pregnant wife?" She'd told us almost everything, but reliving it was a lot for anyone. All of us stayed huddled at the counter as Suzette recounted what happened that night. Even Clark joined to listen."

"Ma-Ma'am, your hus-husband, he know where you are?"

Suzette shook her head. She wiped at a tear in her eye, and shook her head again. "He thinks I am visiting my family out west. I told him that I needed time, and that I'd call when I call. He was so mad, he's still mad, and trying to blame me..." she stopped as an errant sob caught her breath.

"I wish I could smoke in here," she revealed, and laughed. "Boy, that'd set him off." Suzette then became very still, and narrowed her eyes. "Do you *know* what he did? That *son-of-a-bitch*, do you?" she spat out. "When I saw my hair in his hand, I knew he was going to hurt me some more. He was going to hurt my baby. *Our* baby. I knew it, and I knew I had to run. When he wasn't looking, just for a second, I threw a punch and landed my hand on his face as best I could. I'm not strong, but I caught him off guard. I pulled up on the car's door handle, but it was locked. I bloodied his nose. I bloodied it good, and thought that maybe it was broken. And then he got so loud, he was screaming at me, and spitting blood from his lips. When I got the door unlocked, I pushed and got the door open, and then got my feet under me, and... and he hit the gas. My hand was still on the door! The car pulled me straight up into the air," her voice faded, and sounded breathy. Ms. Potts motioned for some water, and I eagerly set up a glass in front of Suzette.

After she sipped at the glass, she nodded, and then continued, "And you want to know what I thought about when my body was flying through the air? I remember this as clear as this glass of water in my hands. I thought about having a husband that I'd give my life for, and for our new baby that I was carrying inside of me. I thought that our child was going to solve us, cure us, and finally make us whole. But, you know what? You can't cure a man like that. You can't cure someone who's broken deep down. That's what I thought about while I was flying through the air," she stopped and thumbed the glass of water, pushing the sweat that beaded up on the outside.

"I landed so hard on my shoulder... so hard. And my baby," she paused, and reached down with her hand over her belly. "My baby landed so hard, too. I can still smell the tires, the burning rubber. He was racing away like a *fucking* coward," she stopped talking, then and sat there with the glass of water, as we did our best to console her. When we tried to offer some words to her, or food, or anything, Suzette waved them off, and only asked if she could sit with us for a while. She stayed with us the rest of our shift.

9

Now that I'd come to believe Jarod Patreu was interested in me, Thursdays had changed entirely. First, I found that I was going to the restroom and looking in the mirror a lot. Second, I caught myself sneaking peaks at my reflection in one of the toasters. The bent metal of the toaster played back a funny, warped face, smiling with huge eyes, a pinched nose, and monster lips. I blinked, and the face winked at me. I giggled at the image; it was comical, and I needed the laugh. And third, I was nervous. For the last year, I worked in the diner with Jarod, but didn't see him: not like a girl would look at a boy. Apparently, he did see me, and my heart swelled at the thought as my palms went clammy.

Could I be with a boy? Should I? I couldn't help but wonder if my new fondness for Jarod was genuine, or if it was because Ms. Potts put the idea in my head. Ideas can sit and fester, and turn into something entirely new and different. I could be annoyed or mad at her, but I wasn't. I found that I liked to think my affection for Jarod was *more* about me than anything else.

I was just a teenager when I last looked at a boy in *that* way. Just a teenager when I last held a boy's hand, or kissed a boy, or did anything with a boy, for that matter. After all this time, could I be with a boy? Or better yet, should I? The questions tugged at me like the April chill that was in the air. Bumping the thermostat's cool setting over to warm, I cursed our loss of the recent stretch of toasty days. Yes, everything is temporary, but I still cursed the spring season setback. The questions bothering me, tugged and nagged some more, and left me wondering if there was a place in this world for me to love again. And whether I deserved to love again. I shook the chill off, and then pushed the questions out of my mind. For now, I decided, the questions weren't for me to answer.

As for Jarod, Ms. Potts didn't think anything of it. She saw a young girl and boy, and let the game of matchmaking begin. But she doesn't know me. She doesn't know about the Gabby that ran from Texas in the middle of the night, the one who ran when it was dark, when the only other things on the road were midnight truckers, and armadillos, and other runaways like me. And she dug. She knew there was more to me than just someone who'd ended up homeless and on the streets.

Part of that is true, though, I did run from Texas. I did travel west, and then north, and then due east. And, during my travels, I met every kind of person under the sun. I walked during the days, and worked odd jobs, and ate whenever I could. And I slept on busses, and under bridges, and sometimes in public restrooms. I slept wherever I found I could lay my head without being beaten, robbed, or raped.

Grabbing a cup and pouring myself some coffee, the cold touch of the ceramic turned warm while I stared into the blackness steaming between my hands. A memory bubble surfaced, like watching someone through a window. I was living in California, and staying in a mobile home that was not so mobile at all. An old shell, a large trailer had been abandoned and left to rust away in a field. A small band of us called it home, and resurrected it, or, at best, we kept it from getting any worse.

I lived with a group of other kids, most of them had run from something, too. There was a code amongst us: *don't ask, don't tell.* And we never did. The trailer we lived in was under the name of someone who'd died a year earlier. As long as we handed over some dollars to the property manager, nobody seemed to care. Nobody ever cared. Nobody asked questions, and nobody came knocking on the screen door.

For a trailer, it wasn't bad – we made a home.

Nothing fancy. The screen door was rusted in spots, and hung from one hinge. It made a terrible metal-on-metal clacking sound when you let it go too soon, but it worked, and kept the outside from the inside. The trailer had old wood paneling for the walls that the kids posted pictures up on, or taped up drawings (some cheerful, some not) and, on occasion, I'd even read a poem from a loose page tacked up. Where we stayed and slept was just the one main room – most of the trailer's walls and kitchen stuff had been taken or stolen. We attached a laundry cord near the ceiling and ran it from wall to wall, hanging sheets in a simple attempt to create some privacy for ourselves.

I liked it. I maybe even loved it. At night, I'd go in my own little sheeted cocoon, ball myself up in my sleeping bag, and listen to the life going on outside the thin walls of the trailer. And, sometimes, I'd listen to the life on the inside of the trailer. I'd hear a few of the other kids whispering to one another, or hooking up, the way kids do. But sometimes I'd hear crying. The kind that you try to hold back, but can't; the kind that stops, as if taking a rest, and then gets going again. The next morning, when pulling our sheeted walls down, we never asked who was crying. We never wanted to. We just went on with our day. *Don't ask, don't tell.* It didn't bother me, especially on mornings when my eyes were still red and sore, and my pillow damp.

Most of us worked as part of a picking crew for the handful of vineyards in the area. To look at a bottle of wine back then, I would never have guessed just how important it was to properly cut the grapes from the vine. A boy named Steve showed me how to do it. I don't recall his last name, but that's not important now. We worked and lived together for a month, and I'd gotten to know him, maybe even liked him a little. He was a cute guy with sandy hair and a dimpled chin. His eyes were sea-green, and I remember him liking to smile a lot. Or maybe he was just smiling when I was around; sometimes it's nice to think that way.

The vines holding the cluster of grapes had a rough feel, and getting used to the shears felt awkward. One slip, and I was sure to cut more than just the grapes. Slow was good. I'd already cut a few grape clusters, and was working on another, when a man came running from between the vines. He was stout, and was wearing an orange vest. He had these tiny bean-shaped eyes that were set all the way back in his head. He was yelling something at me, and I dropped my arms. When he reached me, his round puffy face jiggled while he hollered some more. He took the grape clusters I'd cut out of my hand, and threw them to the ground.

He started darting his tiny bean eyes between the clusters on the ground, me, and the shears in my hand. And when his puffy face began to jiggle again while he shouted, I remember thinking that I was going to laugh. Just burst out laughing. And I think I sort of did laugh a little, but I stuffed it in a mock cough. He scolded another minute, or more, and I tried to apologize, but I think he just liked yelling. Finally, I grabbed another cluster of grapes and began to cut.

Steve approached me from behind, and wrapped his arms around me. I was startled at first, but then felt comfortable. I could feel his heart on my back, and his breath on my neck. He was close. He cupped my hands in his, and with the shears in one hand, we held a cluster of grapes in the other.

"Gentle," he said, and then he showed me how to cut the stem. I liked that his hands were big, and covered mine. They felt strong. Safe. I leaned my body into his, and pulled his arms closer around me as we picked up another cluster of grapes.

"Like this?" I asked, and he breathed a soft reply in my ear,

"Yes, like that." By the third cluster of grapes, puffy face had moved on to yell at someone else, leaving me and Steve to work the row of vines alone. I didn't mind.

That night when we'd all gone to bed, Steve climbed into my sleeping bag. Was I surprised? Maybe a little. But I think I wanted to be with him, and certainly my body was telling me to. I remember how good everything felt. He held me and moved his hands, touching me, as he kissed my neck and my mouth. We helped each other pull our clothes off, and kicked them to the bottom of my sleeping bag. My body was wrapped in his, sweating and heaving, and then it happened. Memories of Texas, and why I had to leave stole the moment from us. I had to push him away. I told him I was sorry. I told him that I couldn't be with him. Steve was a good guy, a gentleman. He didn't call me a prude or a tease. Instead, he kissed my cheek and said that he liked me – that he cared for me, and that he could wait. I kissed him then: a good, hard kiss with regret on my lips. That was the last time I ever saw him.

The next morning, before the day stirred everyone awake, I was back on the road. I'd bundled and packed my things after Steve left my sleeping bag, and waited until I could see the first light reaching up from behind the mountains. I didn't wait until I could see the sun; I only waited for the darkest of the night to start lifting. Leaving the trailer, I remember the cold hitting my face. With a cloudy breath whispered from my mouth, and only a thin jacket to cover me, the first miles were going to be cold. By then, I'd learned to cope with the weather; warm or cold, you wore what you had on you, because that was all you carried. There was no going back inside to change, or to pick up a sweater, or thicker socks and a heavier coat.

Walking that first mile, I was on a road that was just

two lanes. I could see the outline of mountains to the left of me: ominous figures that stayed fixed in the horizon, and would scare me if I let them. Sometimes it was the moon that did it, too. On my right, I could hear the wind rushing over the long grassy fields of the farms and the vineyards. An owl startled me when it screeched a call over my shoulder, and picked something off the road in front of me. When the moon was highest in the sky, the smaller animals liked the warm blacktop of the road. The sun baked the asphalt during the day, and it stayed warm through the night, feeling tepid to the touch by morning.

When the first rays of the sun were a sliver in the horizon, I'd already walked a few miles. It wasn't my first sunrise walk. Might have been my fourth or fifth. It's easy to leave early in the morning. Leaving at night only invites the people you are staying with to try and stop you. Everyone is awake, half of them baked on something, or drunk on something else. But, in the morning, nobody wants to know, or cares to know. Even when they hear you rummaging around, or hear a door open, they might ask what you're doing – you only have to tell them to go back to bed, and they always do.

I liked leaving before the sun came up. It was somewhat symbolic, I thought – a kind of rebirth. In my travels, I learned that the sun doesn't come up like it does on cartoons. There is no funny pop sound as a glowing yellow orb vaults into the sky with a little bounce. Instead, a deep red light bends around the horizon, and reaches into the fields and mountains. As the sun rises, enough of the deep red turns orange and yellow, as the light begins to replace the dark sky. I love the watching the colors change, and sometimes sit on the warm blacktop and stare into the sky. The stars begin to fade, along with the blackest of black. Eventually, there is enough light that you can see your hands and feet, and make out the details of the mountains. When my timing was good for a symbolic rebirth, I could walk a full hour before finally seeing the light turn golden and sharp, and, best of all, my favorite thing: warm.

Texas. There was no wishing that away. There never could be. What's done was done, and I'd moved on. Shaking my head, I pushed memories of home out of my mind. I forced myself to think about Jarod, and felt my cheeks warm. My eyes wandered to the old clock on the wall, where the hour hand approached the number four; only, it was spelled out in the letters. He'd be showing up soon to do his run around the diner, fixing what was broken. He never had to stay for more than an hour or two. And when he did have to stay, he would sometimes come back and finish the next day. A thought crossed my mind... maybe I'd break something that would bring him back tomorrow. I wanted to be closer to him, and see if there was more to this than just Ms. Potts' imagination.

Walking around the counter toward the back, I glanced around the diner, and considered my idea. It was farfetched, and I laughed at the silliness of it, but it wasn't a bad one.

"Help you, G-Gabby?" Clark asked. I flinched, and spun in the direction of his voice. He was quick to raise an apologetic hand, and chuckled, "D-didn't mean to startle you."

"That's okay, should've been paying attention. What do you have, there?"

Clark was resting on his cot, his back against the wall, a blue book in his hands. I'd seen him with the book before. Many times. In fact, it was the only book I think I'd ever seen him reading. The corners of the pages were turned up and out – worn down to mere feathered remains of the paper. The book's binder was creased, and the blue color emptied from it, exposing some of the amber-colored glue, and yellowing threads that held his book together. I tried to read the title, but that, too, had been aged, or rubbed away. I wondered how many times he'd read the book, or leafed through the pages? A quick look around the table, and his cot, and the shallow wall shelf above him: there was just the one book with blue covers, and worn pages.

"J-just reading. Did the b-bell ring? My hearing might be off. Happens sometimes," he asked, and motioned a hand to his ear.

"No, I was just wandering and waiting," I began, and peered out to the front to take a count of tables. "Ms. Potts has just the one table, but they look to be finishing. It's okay; probably won't see anything for another half hour. So, what's your book about?"

"You was j-just *waiting*," he looked at me with a smile, "I know it's Th-Thursday. J-Jarod been crushin' on you." A sudden rush of warmness filled under my collar as I waved off his teasing. Was I the only one who didn't notice this about Jarod? To help push away the embarrassment, I asked again about his book.

"Tell me what you're reading. I've seen it before." A moment passed, and the smile on Clark's face changed. He leaned the back of his head against the wall, and put his hand atop the book, and closed his eyes. At first, I thought he'd fallen asleep. Crazy as that may sound, you come to expect crazy sometimes, when working in a diner. I pushed the thought out when I saw his lips moving. He was saying a small prayer. I couldn't hear it, but that is what I think he was doing.

When he opened his eyes, he glanced at me, and then back to the book. Then he began to speak, and it was different. I couldn't put my finger on it at first, but it was different. His stutter was gone, or almost gone.

"First half of this book is about someone I knew a long, long time ago. A sad story – a painful story. So much hurt and despair. It's a wonder they were able to survive it. The second half of the book shows how they recovered, a g-guidance to living, you might call it. Gabby, this book saved my life. Spent a lot of my early years in and out of trouble. Ended up doing some time, locked up with more of my kind. I was a mad and hateful person."

"Is this what the detective was talking about?" I asked, then wished I hadn't. I didn't want to push, especially when he was sharing. Clark raised a hand, and I understood.

"When I was holed up in prison, full of hate, and spite, and wanting everyone t-to feel the same, I done some bad things a man shouldn't do. But I liked feeling that way. It was like wearing a favorite coat. The hate gets on you like a skin, and you carry it with you, with very breath. I thought it was n-normal. But it wasn't. I was a broken man. You understand?" he asked, narrowing his eyes. I nodded. I didn't understand all of it, but I understood enough. "Gabby, I was the kind of guy you wanted to stay away from. The kind you crossed to the other side of the street when you saw me coming. Shit, I'd trip your grandmother if I thought she'd spill a dime bag. And, if nothing spill, then maybe I'd beat on her, and take what I wanted." He stopped, and I suppose maybe my expression gave him reason to pause. The person in front of me wasn't the man he was describing. Not our Clark. And I couldn't understand how he ever could have been that person. Or maybe I didn't want to understand.

"I'm sorry," I apologized, and nodded for him to continue.

"You sure?" he questioned, and raised his brow. I nodded again.

"Please."

"Six months I spent turning my cell block inside and out, running schemes to help get a fix. I did things I ain't never gonna be able to take back. And then a man come up to me in the yard one day, and asked if I was ready. Just like that, asked if I was ready. I braced for a fight, a *shiv* to my belly, something. When nothing happened, he asked if I was tired of being me. And if I was ready to change. Till that day, I didn't know you could change. Thought n-never crossed my mind. So, I told him sure. Be honest, thought he was holding something – thought he'd be offering it up; a quick fix I could take to pass another couple of hours. He told me to write a list. He said to write down everything I'd done, everything I hated, and everything bad that'd been done to me. And when I was done writing, to bring the list to him.

You ever try and write a history like that? I didn't get it done that night, or the night after. A few weeks it took before I had what he was asking for. But I did it, and I gave it to him. That was the last I'd seen him in near a month."

"Did he work for the warden?" I felt suspicious for Clark, and wondered if there was something more to the list. Clark's eyes widened as he nodded.

"Th-that is what I thought. After a month, I was fixing to hurt him. Hurt him for holding what I'd written down. And when another week went by, I'd decided I was going to go after him. Was going to hurt him bad first, and then stick him. Man come to me a day later, grinning ear to ear. He gave me back my list, folded, same way I gave it to him. He told me he never looked at it – said he didn't need to, he'd seen his own once, and didn't expect much different. He gave it back, and said I needed to take it, to keep it. And he said that, when I was ready, I was to read it. I thought he was practicing some kind of voodoo shit, you see all kinds of weirdness inside them walls.

That night, I pulled my list from my pocket, and opened it slow-like. Had me just enough light to see my scribbles. I was expecting something to drop out, maybe some reefer rolled up in ass paper, or a stamp with the goofy glue on the back. There wasn't anything in my paper – nothing but my pencil scratches. Had just a thin reach of light peeking into my cell, not enough to read by, though.

This is the part I'll never forget. A moonlight finger come in from somewhere up the cell block. It crept across that cold floor of my cell, and then up the cell's wall, and onto my paper. The light landed on the very first thing I'd written down. Later, I come to know that it was God's finger pointing the way for me to see. And, by moonlight, I read my list, but had to stop halfway. It was too much for me to see all at one time. I cried that night. Was the first time in my miserable life I cried."

"Is that the list?" I asked, pointing to the folded paper sticking out of the book. He lifted the book, and rested his hand back on the cover. Touching the paper, he answered,

"Yes. That's it. I ain't never read it again. Not since that night."

"But, why?"

"I keep the list to remind me who I used to be. Time ain't on my side – not up here in Clarksville," he said, tapping his fingers against his head. "Time for me erases everything. Without something to remind me, I'll forget. Can't afford to forget. And I don't ever want to be that person again. After that night, I went to that man, and asked him what he'd done. Man just looked at me with his silly grin again, and asked if I'd read my list. I told him I had, but that I had to stop. He put his hand on my arm, all gentle-like, and told me to meet him later. That afternoon, he gave me this book. He said you ain't never have to feel the way you're feeling. Not ever again. I read this book at l-least once a year."

Questions about the detective and what happened with Ms. Potts were popping up in my head, and I wanted to ask. Even though this was Clark, I still felt nervous. Anxious.

"Did going to prison have anything to do with Ms. Potts? Or Detective Ramiz?" When I asked, Clark didn't say a word. He stood in silence, and put his book back on the shelf. The sound of the book sliding into place seemed to last forever.

Finally, he said, "W-was sharing something with you, Gabby, was all I wanted to do. B-but, I can't share nothing about that," he answered with a look of disappointment. I'd hurt his feelings. Clark opened up to share something so very personal, and instead of listening to him, I went digging, like Ms. Potts had done with me. The nervous rattle inside kicked, and grew into guilt. I know what it is like being on the other side of questions. Questions that you don't want to answer. *There is a time to ask, and a time to listen,* I heard in my head.

"Clark – I'm sorry. I am," I breathed with guilt pressing on my words. He moved, and took a step forward, and I put my hand on his arm. I expected he might push past me, but he didn't.

"Gabby, I wanted t-to share with you with a hope th-that one day, you might share with us. Your family."

"I just wanted to know about Detective Ramiz, and what his interest is in you and Ms. Potts." He sighed, and gestured a brief no.

"C-Can't share that with you," he repeated, and then went to the front.

10

Regret and guilt can be a lethal combination. As I stood by Clark's cot and glimpsed his old book on the shelf, I wanted to kick myself for having opened my mouth. Had I just waited, even for a few minutes, then there would have been time enough to ask what I wanted answered. But I didn't. I sometimes did that; I interrupted conversations, and pushed what was sitting on my tongue and pressing on my lips. And, while I didn't always interrupt, I found that I almost always regretted it when I did.

I heard the bell sound its metal chime from the front, and, before leaving Clark's nook, I heard it ring a second time. One of them belonged to Jarod, I was sure of it. My heart leapt, and worry took my breath as I realized I couldn't do another check. No running to the restroom to check my hair, or finding a toaster to see if I had anything between my teeth. A quick glance around Clark's nook, and I discovered he didn't keep a mirror. Not a one. Was that odd? I considered it for a second, and then saw the empty screen of his TV staring up at me. That would work.

The little white box sat precariously on a makeshift table: a turned-up vegetable crate with ashen gray colors showing the wood's age. The screen was dark, and the face reflecting in the glass was more a silhouette than someone I recognized. But, in the dim gray screen, I could still make out enough of my teeth and my hair, and felt better about the reflection after tucking away a stray lock behind my ear.

My heart bumped again, and I hesitated. What if this feeling was just Ms. Potts putting a bug in me? What if I was growing her idea and feeding on an imaginary crush that really didn't exist? I dismissed the thoughts, and straightened my outfit. Real feelings or not, I didn't think I cared – this was fun.

An air of tension was immediate as I walked to the front of the diner. I felt the grin I'd rehearsed with the RCA's reflection disappear. Two booths were occupied, and a few folks were seated at the counter and getting their first sips of coffee. The inside of our diner felt electric. It was filled with the static air of a storm that rumbled threats and echoed warnings. I thought at any minute lightning would strike down on someone if they moved suddenly, or spoke up too loud.

Somebody called my name, and, when I looked, I saw Suzette at the counter. Nearly healed of all injuries, she looked beautiful; a healthy beautiful. Maybe *too* beautiful. A twinge of jealousy fueled that last thought. Her cheeks were fuller, and flush with color. The dark circles that hung under her eyes were gone completely; their absence forgave five years in her age. And her hair: no more torn patches from her skull to hide – it was a new style for her, and it looked trendy and sexy. It was a new Suzette – maybe she really did leave her husband.

Another jealous pang grumbled in me as I sought out the owner of the second ring of the bell. I loved Suzette, but didn't want to be next to her when Jarod saw me. Instinctively, I groped at the front of my outfit and pulled out any bunching, smoothing as much as I could. As a waitress, there wasn't exactly anything appealing or elegant with what I wore. No sexy outfits. No cleavage to show off, or to help as an attention grabber. And Suzette was the type that could wear anything and still look as though she were modeling it. I felt frumpy again as I grabbed the sides of my outfit and pulled there, too. I hated that feeling.

"Miss Gabriella Santiago," a thick and stony voice sounded from a corner booth. "That is your full name, isn't it?"

A confused look filled Suzette's eyes, replacing the

excited smile on her face. I am sure the same look must have been planted on mine, and, in my next breath, all thoughts of Jarod were forgotten.

"Miss Gabriella Santiago from the little town of Fairview, Texas. Disappeared, it says here – disappeared from her home approximately ten years ago. But, what's this? No missing persons report? So, can it be assumed that you *left* Texas? And why is that, Miss Gabriella Santiago? A runaway? Come on! You look too smart for that. Certainly you would not have considered such a cowardly act." The reciting of my history was cut short when the detective threw his hands over his mouth to catch an explosion of coughs. He grabbed up one of the napkins and coughed a mess of phlegm into it. As he wiped his lips, his shoulders shuddered with another turn of coughs. He coughed again until his body fell forward, his hand keeping his balance on the table top. I thought he was going to pass out. I thought for sure we'd see him face down on the table.

A young couple and child in one booth, and the *Keep on Truckin'* guy at the counter looked up and waited. Nobody offered to help. They waited. These were my regulars. They were Ms. Potts' regulars, too, and the detective had already set a tone. What a way to live; a life where your minutes and hours and days pass with the speculation and accusation of others, filling everyone around you with worry and trepidation.

When the eruption of coughs slowed, I approached the detective and brought another setup along with a clean napkin. Red rivers and creeks forked paths across the whites of his eyes with agitated tears brimming, and then falling onto his cheeks. He pulled the napkin back from his mouth, and asked for some water. There was blood in the linen. He wasn't just coughing up the years of smoking his body was rejecting; there was damage he was paying for.

"So, what is it? What did you run away from in Texas? Was the state not big enough for you?" he joked, and coughed, and then laughed louder while searching for another laugh to join in with his. But nobody said a word.

"Why don't you leave her be?" Ms. Potts scolded. The detective turned his head, the curl on his lips gone, and warned her with a narrowed stab of his eyes. When he was certain Ms. Potts was silenced, he turned back and continued,

"She's a big girl. Miss Gabriella Santiago can answer on her terms. Isn't that right?" I answered a quick yes to him, as I placed the glass of water on the table.

"Truth is, Miss Gabriella Santiago is as clean as clean can be. No felonies, no warrants. Not even a jaywalking charge," he stated evenly. The detective was looking at me. His eyes narrowed again, as if studying a puzzle. "In fact, there hasn't been much of you anywhere in the last ten years. Isn't that right?" he questioned, his eyes widened, waiting for an answer.

"Yes. I suppose that's right. And it's Gabby. Not Gabriella. Just Gabby."

The curl on his lips returned, and he eked out a giggle and chided, "So we're friends now, Miss Gabby? Some pleasantries, and a thank you very much?" The detective sneered, and waited for me to say something. I thought it best to stay quiet. So that is what I did.

"Very well, then," he started to say, "and now that we're all friends, I have something to share." From his coat, the detective pulled a manila envelope, and placed it on the table in front of him. It was old, and the edges had worn to thin cottony frays, like the corners of Clark's book. The light-brown buff paper lay faded, with a heavy crease down the middle. Folded, I thought, and guessed the detective liked to fold the cover back. I could still read the case number penned in blue across a white sticker. But the lettering, too, was fading.

"Do you know what this is?" he asked in his thick, earnest voice, but I remained cautious.

"Case file?" I guessed, and was fairly certain I was right. His eyes brightened, and his earlier smile opened to a full grin, revealing two rows of nubby yellow teeth. One tooth stayed long, and protruded upward like a dying tree. In that moment, his upturned face resembled a badger with a toothy grin.

"Perceptive. I like that. This is my *last* case file. My only remaining unsolved crime. And it has everything to do with your friends over there, Clark and Ms. Potts. So, given we're all friends now, I thought I'd fill in some of the details for you." I took a step back from the table as he opened the case file. Regret surfaced again from interrupting Clark. I turned once to Clark, his face was statue-like, and his eyes stared at us, but I could see they were far away. Ms. Potts had moved to a stool and sat down. She'd raised her hand to her mouth, as though trying to hold in her words. At some point, the young couple must have decided a real-life police drama was too exciting. They decided that it wasn't as safe to watch in person as it was on television. They picked themselves up and left.

Suzette remained. Her eyes were moving from person to person, and I wondered what she must be thinking. Maybe, when the air in the diner became electric, Suzette froze. Maybe, on some subconscious level, or from instinct, or just self-preservation, she knew to do that. This was one of her senses – we all have it, but she'd come to rely on it.

The detective must have read the look on my face. He must have known I was in the dark about such things, and empty of all knowledge of his final case.

"Ahhh," he coughed out, and then grabbed the bloodied napkin to cover his mouth. When the threat of more coughing passed, he looked at me, and asked, "They haven't told you, have they? They haven't told you about the murder. How very interesting." Again, he showed his nubby teeth in a grin. I didn't want to move, or say or do anything, but I did. I gave a short nod of my head. Detective Ramiz stood up, and stepped out from the booth. Taking off the fedora from atop his head, he plopped it on the table next to the open case file. Papers ruffled and lifted, and threatened to fall to the floor. I hoped they would. I'd spill something on them if they did. But the pages settled, and the detective spoke.

"Ms. Potts," he began, and stepped in her direction. Like a moth turning away from the heat of a flame, she leaned closer to the counter, away from the detective. "Ms. Potts, where is your husband? Where is Mr. Louis Potts?" he asked, as he approached, and then waited, standing in front of her. Married? Had I heard him correctly? I'd never considered there to be a Mr. Potts. Or maybe I had, but just assumed he passed on long ago. The detective pushed himself up on his toes, and then back, slamming his heels to the floor. Ms. Potts flinched at the sudden sound. "Come now Ms. Potts – Mr. Louis Elmore Potts. Your husband of –" he paused, and tapped the side of his head, "forty years? Yes. Forty years. But, the last time you saw him, or anyone saw him, was twenty years ago."

"My husband is dead. You know that," Ms. Potts

blurted. She quickly bumped up the thick frames of her glasses, and continued, "Dead twenty years now, God rest his soul. But we told you this a dozen times before. Why can't you just leave it be?"

"Well, sure, official reports list him as dead. Even that case file could be closed, if I let it. But at one time, your husband was a missing person. *You* had him declared dead. Never found a body, though, did we?"

"If my husband were alive, he'd be with me. But he ain't," Ms. Potts stated, and put her hand back in front of her mouth.

"Only a matter of time – Angela's will be sold. Interest is heating up, and they're not keeping your precious diner. Did you know that, Ms. Potts? How about you, Clark?" The detective continued, raising his gravelly voice. "They're not going to preserve or rescue your safe haven for the likes of convicts and runaways and *dead bodies*," he declared, passing his eyes to me and Clark. The detective's expression went flat and exacting: he intended to close his last case.

The tension and strain bled a congestion that was thick and ugly, and it overwhelmed Ms. Potts. She bolted from where she sat, and faced the detective. Fear struck me as I thought she was going to hit him – cartwheel her short arms, and swing them down on him. But she stopped herself. She faced him with a stern expression and pensive eyes.

"You don't know! You don't know me and Clark and this *safe haven*! My husband is dead! Ain't nothing more to know than that! So, take your *last case,* and..."

"Ms. Potts!" the detective yelled, "I haven't finished. Now, if you would," he stressed, and motioned his hand to the stool behind her. The fiery expression she had moments before faded, as though in a classroom that had been reprimanded by the principle. Ms. Potts took a reluctant step back, and sat on the stool. This wasn't fair. It wasn't right. The detective had a vendetta that was fueled by some notional theory about a man who'd disappeared twenty years ago. That is what I thought, anyway, before hearing more of what he had to say.

Detective Ramiz coughed a new butterfly-splatter of blood and phlegm onto the white linen. He studied it a second, and found me staring, too. He snapped the napkin into a fold, and tucked it into his pocket. I could see he was afraid. He might have seen butterfly blood spatters a dozen times a day – every one of them scared him some. More than that, I could see that he knew he was running out of time. He shrugged, as if to say it was nothing, and then turned to face Clark.

"And Clark, you've been here almost as long as Ms. Potts. If my memory serves, that back room of yours wasn't always there. Was it? Angela Thurmon bumped it out and put on that addition." The detective walked around the counter, and stood opposite of Clark. When

Clark said nothing and only offered a vacant stare, the detective took a cup from the back counter, and poured himself some coffee. We watched him drink half of the cup without so much as a wince of his eyes, or a flinch in his face. Hot and black. He drank the fresh coffee straight – when he brought the cup down from his mouth, steam rolled up over his lips like a dragon's breath. The sight of him with his badger grin and coffee steam bleeding from his mouth was sinister, if not downright frightful.

"Let me ask you something. Back then, before the addition, what stood behind you, Clark? Hmmm? Don't know? Maybe this will help. I used to sit right there, where Ms. Potts is sitting now, and she'd serve me up two eggs and a side of bacon. And I used to see you working the grill back there, and the only thing *I* could see behind you were some... what was it?"

"Sh-Shelves. J-Just some shelves, is all. N-Nothing else."

"Right as rain, son. Nothing else. Nothing but a wall, and a door out to the back of the building. Angela Thurmon had grand plans, and bumped all of it out for refrigerators and a dishwasher. Not the kind you buy for your home – these were the big ones, big and professional." The detective poured the remaining coffee down his throat, and let out a steam-filled *ahhhh* that rose and disappeared like smoke just beyond his lips.

"When you build in big appliances, you have to add

all sorts of plumbing and electricity. Don't you? Angela Thurmon had to dig new trenches to tap into the water lines. For a while, it looked like a moat back there. Didn't it? Deep one, too. Wasn't it? But they cleaned it up all nice and pretty-like. Poured in that concrete pad you're standing on now. Didn't they?"

"I-I suppose? Yes. Y-Yes, they did," Clark answered, and looked briefly at the detective, but then turned away. Ms. Potts held her hand to her mouth, and Clark glanced at me, but again turned away. The detective spun around to face the front like a lawyer in a courtroom, facing a jury.

"Mr. Louis Elmore Potts was last seen entering Angela's Diner. Eye-witnesses from the Irish Pub saw him leave the bar, walk up the street, and enter the diner. Mr. Louis Elmore Potts was never seen again. Clark... just when did they pour the pad?" he asked, leaning his head over his shoulder in Clark's direction.

"Pad?"

"The concrete," the detective raised his voice, "When did they pour the floor you're standing on?"

"D-Dunno, not too g-good with dates," Clark answered, and shrugged his shoulders.

"That's okay, I can fill in the blanks for you. It was the next day. The very next day. Isn't that right, Ms. Potts – I know *you* know the date. You reported him missing on that day. Just one day. Not two, or three, or five?

Nope, one day. And that, my dear was a mistake. Raised suspicions at the station right away."

"But he always come home. No matter what his business was at the pub. My husband always come home to me," Ms. Potts finally said. Her voice shook as she spoke, and her hands trembled. She pulled her hands together when she saw me watching. She pulled them together, as though praying. The detective turned away from his imaginary jury to face Ms. Potts. His eyes gleamed, and his face looked younger, more vibrant. He welcomed the rebuttal. He orchestrated it. He wanted to hear the contradiction so that he could put Ms. Potts on the spot.

"I know. I've heard you say that before. In fact, it is in my case file over there on the table. But, you know what else is in my case file? A report stating that you and Clark were the only two people working in the diner that night. Convenient? And the next morning, men in big trucks rolled down this narrow street, and poured the concrete. Did anyone look in the trenches? Was there an inspection before the pour?" the detective finished. I waited a second to hear more, but the brightness in his eyes dimmed, and the vibrant excitement on his face faded. He was spent. He clutched at his chest and sucked in air – I could hear crippled rattling in his chest as another flurry of coughs threw him forward. A moment passed, and the quiet in the diner was replaced with the shuffling sound of the detective's shoes as he made his way back to his booth.

"You see, Gabby... we're still friends, right? My last case, my remaining case, is as real as any missing persons case. And the shared opinion is that this has always been a case of murder," he finished in the same tone that he started. A loud wheezing sound came from his mouth, and he began to fall forward. He reached out and clutched the table for support. We all passed looks back and forth, and I wondered if there were images in their heads of the detective falling over and dying. When he composed himself once more, he placed his fedora back on his head, and unrolled a few dollars from his hand.

"Your tip is for bringing me the water. That was a civil thing to do; very civil of you... amongst friends," he grinned, "and the extra dollars are for you to call home. Call your parents. Children should be civil to their parents." Holding the dollar bills in the air, he waved them, and then dropped the collection to the table. And, like before, the bell above the door rang out, and seemed to clear the electricity in the air. But did it? Could it? The detective talked of murder. He accused Clark and Ms. Potts of murder.

11

When Detective Ramiz left the diner, I turned to face Ms. Potts, and wanted to scream, *Is it true? Is any of it true?* But I couldn't. The thought of any of this, all of it, was overwhelming. As I considered the breadth of the detective's accusations, I thought I'd start to cry. I mean, this was my new family, my home, and the two angels who'd saved my life a year ago might be falling from heaven right in front of me. The faint sound of the bell above the door pulled my attention – we were alone. A part of me wanted a full diner: a busy diner. A diner full of life that I could hide in and not be concerned about what I'd just heard.

"Gabby, you don't need to worry yourself with any of this. We've known the detective for the better of twenty years, now. And we answered his questions already; more than a few times," Ms. Potts explained, but her voice lacked the same confidence as her words.

"I heard the detective," I began, "We all heard him. And he wasn't here just to give you a hard time. He has a plan. I don't know exactly what it is, but whatever it is he has, he has more of it now, and I don't think he is going to stop."

"M-Ma'am, do you think G-Gabby right?" Clark questioned, and was immediately met by a loud *shhhh,* as Ms. Potts raised her hand in his direction. But Ms. Potts regarded what Clark said as worry creased her brow. She closed her eyes, and began to rock back and forth.

"Ma'am?" Clark implored. Ms. Potts raised her hand again, and tightened her eyes shut, as though running from the questions in the darkness. She continued to rock back and forth.

"Ma'am – can't go back to prison," Clark whimpered. Ms. Potts stopped rocking and opened her eyes with a deep sigh. She pushed her glasses back, and looked at me and Suzette, and then Clark.

"I know it, Clark. I've known it these last twenty years. Ain't nobody known it like I do. Baby, you..." her words stopped, and she heaved in air and began to cry.

"I don't know what happened. But, does it still matter – does it matter anymore?" Suzette muttered, "I mean, the detective's entire case seems to hinge on an eye-witness account of Mr. Potts being here, in the diner."

"M-Miss Suzette, he *was* here that n-night. And s-so was w-we," Clark stammered, and I could see he was shaken badly. Scared. Clark began to move his lips like he had earlier. He was praying. Only, now he was praying for more. Something did happen that night, and both Clark and Ms. Potts were involved. I hated thinking of them in this light; it was surreal and almost impossible to comprehend. Could they have been part of a murder?

"So, something happened? What?" I insisted, and heard frustration in my voice. I'd never before talked to Ms. Potts or Clark like that.

Ms. Potts was taken aback by my tone, and stopped crying. She remained quiet another minute, and then poured herself a cup of coffee. She walked to the back, where Clark continued praying, and wrapped her arms around him. He collapsed against her and gave her a weary look.

"I'm tired, ma'am, b-been sitting on this so long." Ms. Potts took his face in her hands, and whispered a long *shhhh*.

"Clark, I don't know what will become of us, but maybe it is time. Maybe we been sitting on this thing long enough," she said in a somber voice that sounded hoarse and tired. Clark mouthed another prayer, as Ms. Potts joined him. When they finished, he glanced at me and Suzette.

"Maybe things happen this way for a reason. Maybe

you c-can help?"

I walked behind the counter, and stood opposite of Suzette, whose eyes furrowed with concern. Ms. Potts came back around to the front, and fixed another cup of coffee.

"Order of coffee and tears," she half laughed, and lifted her cup to us as a tear wet her cheek. When she was ready, she sat on the stool and told us their story. With an empty diner and a full pot of coffee, Ms. Potts told us everything.

Both Suzette and I listened. What was important to her was to first tell us who her husband was. Until now, he was just a name, a name from the mouth of Detective Ramiz. No face. No memory. Not even a description. Just a name. Ms. Potts' expression was one of fondness, as she told how they'd met at a church function. She told us how they were smitten with each other from the beginning. He courted her, and she knew he was the one she would marry; the one who she would spend the rest of her life with.

She told us that he only showed her the good side, the one that brought flowers, and opened doors, and was caring and loving. There was no hint of a man who could hurt her, or a man who was filled with more ugly than any one person should have. He only showed her a side of him that she would fall in love with, and she did. They married in the spring, in the same church they'd met at.

They honeymooned like other couples, and set up a home like other couples, and began to build a life like other couples.

Something changed after their first year. Ms. Potts told us that someone else moved in and became her husband. He was cold and dark, and brooded most evenings. His eyes were different. They were distant one minute, and on fire with anger the next. She told us that she learned to avoid the moods. She avoided the hurtful things he'd say. But she could get him back. She had a plan to get them back to where they were when it was easy and fun, and filled with passion and love.

A fine dinner she'd prepared: one with a cut of steak that he liked, and a decorated plate of sides that were all his favorites. She remembered cooking all afternoon, and even enlisted the help of some friends to make it a night to remember. She waited eagerly to see his smile as he took his first bite.

He only nodded glumly, and said it was okay, but that it was nothing special. He said that maybe she should've cooked up something better. She told him that it was his favorite, and that is when it happened the first time. Her husband hit her with the back of his hand. She never even saw him lift it. A white light streaked across her eyes, and a low tone of ringing settled in her ears. He hit her a second time, and she tumbled to the floor, where she lay, dazed, blinking at the empty ceiling. She said she didn't know what had happened until she felt the food on her. He was screaming, and throwing the meal she'd prepared for him from the table down onto her. He screamed for her to eat it, eat it all, if she was so proud of the slop she'd made for him.

Life changed after that night. There were more attacks, some worse than others. But she stayed. A few attacks left her without the use of her legs. She'd spend a day, sometimes two, in bed, crawling to the bathroom when the need was there. A limp would cripple her walk for a week or more afterward. Other attacks left her eyes bruised and swollen shut to the world. But she stayed. This was her marriage, and her husband, and her vows were for better or for worse.

"But not for the *abused*," Suzette mumbled, her voice lifting angrily.

"He killed my baby," Ms. Potts rasped, and looked at Suzette. "He never knew I was with child. Never knew it all. Not sure his knowing would have stopped him from kicking me across the floor, though. He might've even kicked a little harder," she continued, and stopped long enough for the pain of the memory to pass. "After that, I learned you can't wrestle with a meanness like that. Ain't no praying it away with a Pastor, when they saying: '*It's in God's hands, deary, now pass the basket*'. Whatever gripped my husband and made him who he was, it had him long before I ever met him. He just kept it buried.

Ain't nothing stay buried forever."

I felt a pinch in my gut when Ms. Potts stopped to refresh her coffee. Suzette's eyes were moist, and I was only vaguely aware that she'd reached across the counter to hold my hand. It was cold with perspiration. As Ms. Potts told us about her husband and the kind of man he was, I realized how this was the exact life Suzette was living now. The bruises, the broken bones. The shattered dreams of a family – of a baby. But this time, the pain wasn't by the cruel hand of her husband, James, this time it was through Ms. Potts' words.

When Ms. Potts continued, she talked about that night her husband disappeared. She left none of the details hidden for us to uncover. I could imagine it all, as though I were in the diner with them twenty years earlier. I'm sure Suzette could see it, as well, and more than once, I had to assure her it would be okay.

Mr. Potts entered Angela's Diner like a rushed cold invading the corners of a room. His step was crippled by his favorite drink: whiskey. Ms. Potts didn't have to guess where her husband had been. It was obvious. Mr. Potts drank his fill at the pub across from the diner. He visited earlier than some, and stayed later than most. And, on many nights, he staggered home, but some nights he didn't. On a few occasions, she found him on their stoop, his clothes wet with morning dew, or with the sour smell of his urine.

"I need some money, babe," he struggled to spit out – but his words fell shamelessly to the floor.

"Coffee, instead – maybe?" she offered. There was a reservation... a hesitation in her voice. Caution was carried in her words. By now, she'd learned to temper what she said; short answers only. Too much could set him off.

"I said, I need money!" he raised his voice, and staggered to the counter. When he reached the cash register, he began pushing buttons. His fingers stabbed at the machine as he tried to open the cash drawer. Taking no aim, he stabbed and pushed with confused direction. The display window atop the cash register popped numbers up a few at a time until they jammed. He stabbed his fingers in the air again, and then made a fist and punched the face of the register. Numbered buttons broke and flew off to expose their metal posts.

"Won't open. Gotta open this," he snapped. Ms. Potts took a step forward and watched his hand rise and fall.

"Baby, you can't do that. You can't have the diner's money. Here, take my money," she started to say, and held out a few dollars in change that she'd collected in tips. "Go back to the bar, and I'll see you when I get home. Here, take it," she continued. But even slowed by the whiskey, Ms. Potts didn't see his other hand coming. He swung a closed fist upward, connecting under her extended hands. Tip money flew across the diner, as he let out a cruel laugh, and pushed her back with a punch to her chest. Ms. Potts was thrown, but caught herself on the counter.

"I don't want your dimes and nickels, you stupid ugly woman. Got a poker game, a big one. Gonna use what's in here and put it back later," he guffawed. Ms. Potts knew there was no later. He'd lose the money, all of it. His laugh faded as he began to punch at the register. When Ms. Potts got back to her feet, blood sprayed over her glasses. Her vision was blocked by drops of blood as it raced down the lens of her glasses, and fell from the frame. Her heart raced as she reached and padded her hands around her body, looking for the wound. Her breathing quickened as fear grew, and her hand closed around her face and head, searching for the source of the blood. Another spay hit her across her cheek and neck. She cleared her glasses, and saw that it was her husband's hand. He'd torn open his skin and broken one his knuckles as he'd thrashed a flurry of throws on the face of the cash register.

"No!" she yelled, and stepped in to pull his arm up. When he looked at her, it was with mad eyes. Her husband was nowhere to be found. He was gone. She saw her reflection in the black of his eyes, where the anger and the pain lived, and it almost killed her. Literally. Before she knew what was happening, his hands were around her neck, and her body was bent over the counter. At once, all the air in the room was gone. It was replaced by the squeezing of his hands on her throat. The floor beneath her was gone, and she kicked in a desperate struggle to run. She felt her feet connecting with his legs, and her heels breaking the coffee mugs and tall fountain glasses innocently standing on the shelves beneath her. The light in the diner began to dim as pressure stabbed at her lungs. Pain in her chest grew until she thought she'd explode. The last thing Ms. Potts remembered seeing was the rage in her husband's eyes as he leaned in with his face just above hers, screaming ugliness, while laughing at her. She was dying.

"When I come to, I couldn't stand. Took me five minutes, maybe more, before I could catch a decent breath without coughing it out," Ms. Potts continued, and reached a hand out toward Clark. He was already coming to the front, and put his hand in hers. "My husband tried to kill me. Would've too, but Clark... he saved my life."

"What happened?" I blurted.

"I couldn't speak; he stole my voice with his hands. Nothing come out, but whispery words. I remember crying and wanting to scream when I saw my husband. He was on the floor, right here where I'm standing. His head was opened up like a melon, and lying in a pool of blood. I remember thinking that his blood looked dark. It looked dead, and I wondered if a meanness was something that could be in your blood."

"Clark?" I asked, and he closed his eyes and nodded.

"C-Couldn't let him do it. I was out back having a sm-smoke when I heard the cash register. Awful, terrible noise that kept crashing. Didn't know what it was. By the t-time I come in, he already have Ms. Potts over the counter, just choking the life out of her."

Suzette's hand was shaking, her other hand feeling around her neck, as though reliving what Ms. Potts told us. "My husband choked me once. He choked me on our bed. He said I made him do it, and that it was my fault. I remember thinking *this is how it feels to drown*. When your breath is gone, and everything becomes gray, and all the sounds shrink away somewhere distant," she said, and then looked at Clark. "What did you do?" She asked. Clark passed a look to Ms. Potts, and then to his hand, before settling his eyes on us.

"When I come back in and saw M-Ms. Potts and her husband on top of her, I didn't know what to do. When I saw her feet stop k-kicking and heard him laughing, I picked up my skillet and hit him. Man tumbled down onto the ground like a sack of potatoes. I only hit him once. But it k-killed him. I ain't proud of what I did, just couldn't let him hurt Ms. Potts," he finished, as Ms. Potts embraced his hand in hers.

"Clark, here, is mo' than just our cook," Ms. Potts said, looking up at him. She pulled their hands against her heart, and forced out the words: "He is my angel... and I go to my grave protectin' him." She wrapped her small arms around his middle.

This was their secret. The remaining details that had been told by the detective were eerily similar. He'd done his job. And that thought made me sad and scared for them. Detective Ramiz pieced together the accounts from the patrons at the Irish pub as Ms. Potts' husband left that night to meet his wife at the diner. The detective even had a timeline, as he called it, that placed her husband at given locations, and at approximate times. And these, too, were accurate.

What happened to Mr. Potts next was the mystery. It was the void in the case that kept Detective Ramiz up at night. It led him back here to Angela's Diner, and he wanted the case closed before the cancer eating away at his insides destroyed him.

"And the concrete? The pipes, and the new addition? All true?" I questioned. Ms. Potts let go of Clark.

"Yes. All of it. Clark was on parole from Holmesburg prison. Saving my life was just a minor detail. He killed a man. He'd surely go back to Holmesburg for the rest of his life. I couldn't let that happen. I loved my husband, I surely did. But the man that lay dead in front of us, that wasn't my husband. Not anymore."

"C-Concrete was coming in the m-morning. We took Mr.Potts, and p-put him in the b-back."

"When Clark put him down, I climbed down into the trench with them, and we covered my husband up with stone and dirt. Nobody would know he was there 'less they was looking."

Suzette crunched her face, and asked, "So, your husband is still here? In the floor?"

"Y-yes, ma'am, and I stay here. Died by my hand, and I pray for my soul every day." Clark answered with sadness in his voice.

"Some days, I wished I'd died that night. I wished when the room went gray and then black, that I died. My husband would've gotten what was coming to him at Holmesburg, and Clark would be free. But, I suppose, that ain't how God saw fit for this to play it out."

"That is why the detective is back. The diner's sale! The construction!" I yelled, realizing exactly what the detective meant when he brought up the sale of the Angela's.

"T-Tearing down the diner, they might dig, and if they do that, then they'll find Mr. Potts, and we'll g-go to prison. I can't go b-back," Clark cried in a soft voice, his face littered in fear.

"Then we just can't let that happen. Can we?" Suzette declared. Ms. Potts fixed her glasses.

"I appreciate the thought, but the detective is set in his ways to see this through. He is after us like we's just rodent prey."

The reality of what was being faced was daunting, if not impossible. I liked having answers, but had none. Ms. Potts' husband was buried in the floor of the diner, and the detective was eager to dig it up. And, if he got his way, then my friends would be going to prison. If I were living in a trailer or a tent, I'd be looking at the clock about now, and waiting for the sun to wake the day. An hour before the first rays of sunlight peeled away the night sky, I'd be on the road walking. But this was family. My family. I didn't look at the clock. I didn't look at the road outside. I stayed where I sat, and, as Clark's lips moved to a new prayer, I joined him.

12

For the next week, life at the diner felt somewhat normal. Of course, the idea that a dead body was in the floor beneath Clark's nook was strange – I'm guessing that is where they put Mr. Potts. Strange or not, the diner continued to function. And whether I did or didn't know about the body didn't mean a thing to the person waiting for their coffee. But, now and then, the thought of it did give me the willies, and reason to pause. Would I have done the same as Clark, given the circumstance? Yes. In fact, I think I would have done more. Certainly there was no judgment from me. Fear, however, there was plenty of – especially with the prospects of Angela's Diner being sold, and what Detective Ramiz was after.

Life stayed the norm at Angela's Diner. My regulars came in. They ordered their meals and their coffee, just as they had the days, weeks, and months prior to my learning anything about a dead body. And, for regulars like *Keep on Truckin´*, polishing off his third cup of coffee, how was he to know? He winked at me as he let out a hearty burp. Dropping a few dollars on the table, he wished me well, and told me he would be back in a couple of days: had to drive a load of plumbing supplies down in Virginia, or something like that.

People came and went. They gave appreciative smiles almost as often as they complained. They tipped good and bad. The hours and days moved along no differently than before. I suppose that is how Clark and Ms. Potts managed it – how they moved into every day. For them, it was a matter of life or death. And, even then, people were still going to come in and order the same meal they ordered the day before.

Sometimes, when I was alone, and Angela's was empty and quiet, I'd close my eyes and think about the body in the floor. I'd sit and lay my hands down on the cool surface of the table, and try to feel something, anything. I wondered, if I concentrated enough, would I be able to sense that there was a dead person with us? Would I feel a dead heart beat thumping beneath my feet and echoing in my head?

A part of me was glad I never felt anything. But I'll admit to being a bit disappointed, too. It was a silly thought, and I blamed it on my high-school days and reading Edgar Allen Poe's *Tell-Tale Heart*. Standing from the table, I was relieved the only things I sensed were the comings and goings of cars, and people outside the diner's window. A few times, I caught myself looking down at my feet. No Chuck Taylors, just my waitress shoes pushing on the light green tiles, and I'd imagine a body lying there. Instinctively, I'd step over what wasn't really there.

It would have been Ms. Potts who was killed that awful night, if not for Clark having saved her. I never let myself forget that. I considered this, and wondered where I would be today if Ms. Potts hadn't taken the help wanted sign from my hands. Where would I have ended up? Would I still be living on the streets? And who might have been standing in her place? Would they have blue hair, too, and thick glasses that needed to be pushed up every five minutes? Would they have offered me a meal sprinkled with magic? Would I be alive?

Today was Thursday, and I wasn't racing to see my reflection in a toaster, or to the bathroom mirror to check my teeth and hair. My one minute of infatuation for Jarod Patreu had slipped. Sadly, it may have been squashed. He never showed up last week, which was fine, given the revelation about Ms. Potts' husband. But still, when the bell rang, my eyes popped up to see who was coming in. I felt a smile on my face; what's wrong with that? Suzette met my eyes with a returned smile, and then frowned at my disappointment; I waved it off as nothing. She told me she stopped in to pick something up. And, as quickly as she was here, she was leaving. But not before crossing her fingers while waving a hand in the air and saying that she'd be back to join us later, when it was a little busier.

Suzette's days were much like mine. She even started helping out at the diner. Nothing permanent, just a few hours a day here and there to earn some dollars. When she left her husband, she didn't leave a forwarding address. She'd told him she was visiting family or something like that, but decided, instead, to disappear. To vanish completely. I could help her with that. Disappearing was easy; remaining so could be hard work, and took some care. With a few dollars, anyone can live anywhere they want and never be found. Disappearing is easy: I know.

When Suzette ran from their home, she took with her some clothes, a handful of cash, and the pearls her husband had given to her. That was all she had to work with. It wasn't much, but it was something to get started with. She'd told her husband the pearl necklace had been lost on the streets around Pennypack Park, lost when he dragged her body with the pull of his car, throwing her to the ground, and nearly ending her life. And, she told us, her husband never said a word to her about losing their baby.

An eager gentleman from the pawn store a few miles

away offered to buy the pearls. With a toothy grin and a whistle in his words, he said they were a fine string of natural whites, and that he would pay almost top dollar. When Suzette hesitated, Toothy voiced a disappointment, and then whistled a sweeter offer, by throwing in some store credit, too. She took him up on the sale and used the cash to pay for a room next to Ms. Potts. The pearls were gone, and in their place, she had cash in hand, and a kitty-cat clock whose tail and eyes moved in a count of the seconds. As she put it, the clock made her new room homier. I didn't think so, though. I thought the clock was just creepy.

As Suzette left the diner, I heard a distant rumbling sound from outside as sunlight bounced off a passing car. Sun and thunder – an exciting mix. Spring storms toyed with us most afternoons, and they gave me a perfect opportunity to take a break and watch from the diner's stoop: storm junkie, through and through.

I followed Suzette through the door, where I saw a deep purple curtain approaching from the west. Razor-thin lightning pierced the center; some accompanied by thunder, and some without. More rumbles held promise for a good storm, and I could see sheets of rain spilling. In a few minutes, the rains would be overhead, soaking the diner. We were in the throes of spring weather, and I could taste the warm dampness of the air. Electric.

The bell above the door rang as I entered, and I was

quickly joined by Brown, who was holding the arm of a tall boy. They gave me a smile, and made their way to a booth. He was a boy a few grades older than Brown, and was sporting the same color hair, and a cute pair of dimples when he smiled at her. It had been a while since I'd seen any of the teenage girls. Walking past the fast-food joint, I did see them through the windows now and again, and, once, got a nod and a small wave from Brown and Black. The kids said a quick hello to me; the boy's voice was low, but hitching, as if stuck in an adolescent change. The two collapsed back into each other as they went on chatting a teenage language I once knew.

A giddy feeling lifted me. Brown and her beau had a secret, and it was all over their faces. A sunburn on her nose and cheeks had all but hidden some of her freckles. The same sun painted a faint red burn across his nose and the back of his neck. My guess was that the two had cut class for the day, and had spent the morning and afternoon together. Could this be the infamous Jimmy Taylor? The subject of the near-pregnancy experience shared by Brown and Blonde and her other friends? I suspected it was, and would have to let Ms. Potts in on it and share the table with me.

The two ordered a plate of fries and a milkshake, a favorite of the teens. The milkshake, of course, was for dipping the fries into. The kids thought they came up with the idea, but I knew better. I gave Brown a wink and raised a brow in her friend's direction. She gleamed, smiling wide, and pulled his arm closer to her. The bell rang out, and pulled my attention from the young love.

A man entered the diner and stood for a moment to look to the four corners of the diner. Sizing up our small place, he glanced around the front, and stretched his neck to see the back, and then looked to the counter. He was tall and fit, and wore a suit and shoes that were expensive and probably tailor-fitted. Certainly not something off the rack, or a suit that came with a buy one, get two free weekend sale.

Handsome, the man wore an air of confidence as he made his way to the counter. I could tell he'd never been to Angela's Diner before. It wasn't just that I'd never seen him; he was looking around and taking in all that we had. When he reached the counter, he leaned up on his feet to get a better view of the back, stretching to see everything. He was searching, and I wondered if he might be one of the possible buyers of Angela's Diner. If that was true, that meant Mr. Thurmon might be stopping in. I pushed a small reminder in my head to clean up a bit.

When Handsome was satisfied in not finding or seeing whatever it was he was looking for, he took to one of the stools and sat down. I made my way back to the counter, and put in the order for the fries and a milkshake. And, of course, I had to pass Handsome on the way. He smelled good – not sure what it was, but it slowed my step as I passed him. Twice. Up close, he was even more attractive. And, when he planted his eyes on me and smiled, an unexpected settling of nerves caught my breath with an *ummm* as I asked if he'd like something to drink. My neck felt hot, and I was sure I must have been blushing.

"Just coffee, Miss," he answered, and ran his fingers through his hair.

A nervous giggle crept to my lips, and I felt silly: middle school silly. I poured him a cup of coffee, and waited as he fixed it with a packet of sugar and some creamer. He gave me another polite smile, and then took a sip. I watched his lips. My eyes were drawn to them, and how he sucked in the coffee. It was silly, but he was so handsome. Another thump of nerves played inside me, and I pushed my mouth to say something.

"Coffee is fresh," was all I could stumble out. "Do you like it?"

"Not bad, it's good," he thanked me, and I was caught by his blue eyes. They were bright, very bright; the kind you see in newborns and younger kids. Only, his never changed. They were beautiful.

"Can I get you anything else?" I asked, as Handsome sipped at his coffee again and shook his head a brief no.

"Just passing through, and needed to sit for a few minutes."

"Pick-up," Clark called as I tried to think of

something to say. Clark sounded out another, "Pick-up," when Handsome pointed toward Clark. I told him I'd be back in a few to check on him.

When the teens were settled in with their fries and milkshake, I went back to see how Handsome was doing.

"Can I get you another cup of coffee?"

"That would be fantastic, yes," he answered, and grinned as nerves threatened another giggle. I was feeling silly, but then his smile faded, and his eyes strayed far while he held his coffee.

"Are you here on business?"

He hesitated a moment, then pulled out a blue paper from inside his jacket. The paper's color matched his eyes, and had been folded down the middle where a crease interrupted some of the letters bleeding through. He drummed his hand against the paper, and I could see a heaviness in his eyes. At that moment, the handsome he came in with was gone like the fast move of the spring rains I'd seen approach earlier. His expression was something more familiar. Something we're used to seeing at Angela's Diner. *An Order of coffee and tears,* I heard Ms. Potts yelling in my head. I glanced across the diner to the booth where she was sitting. Ms. Potts was busy working a crossword. She was deep into the newspaper's little boxes, penciling mad scratches, and not looking anywhere but down. Just a glimpse is what I needed from her – a glimpse to use our secret waitress language, to say *come on over here, might have a story for ya to hear*. But she didn't look up.

"Lost my wife," Handsome started to say, swiping at a tear from his cheek.

"I'm sorry, was she sick?"

He shook his head, and drummed the paper with his hand again.

"Sorry, no – not sick. She left, and then disappeared," he explained, and sipped his coffee.

A mystery! I was intrigued, and sought out Ms. Potts one more time, but she still had her head down with her pencil top waving around in small arches and circles. I'd have to fill her in on this one later.

"How long has she been missing?"

"It's been a few weeks. I know she was fond of this area, so I thought I'd ask around. This is my wife," he answered, and then opened the sheet of paper in front of me. The sound of paper crinkling pulled my eyes down, and my heart dropped. I threw a look to Ms. Potts, pleading that she looked up from her damn crossword. I looked back down at the paper, where a photo of Suzette stared back at me. Her face was printed in a mass of shaded blue dots, the large crease running down the middle of her head. Her image held harrowed eyes, and, beneath them, an expressionless smile. The photo looked frightful. Beneath Suzette's face was the printed text of her first name, her age, and a small description. This was her husband sitting across from me, the man who regularly beat on her. The man who'd killed her unborn child. The man who'd driven her to run and hide. My breath was gone, and my legs felt wobbly as I searched for Ms. Potts again.

"May I please leave this flyer with you, and ask that you contact me if you see my wife?" The giddy feeling I had earlier went cold, and, in its place was a growing fear that had already taken my legs. A nervous sweat on my neck caused a chill to run through me, and I told myself to calm down – to take a breath. He held the flyer in front of me, and pushed it in my direction. His hands were enormous. They were huge and thick and dangerous. In my mind, I could imagine seeing him push Suzette down and hitting her. I could almost hear it. Reaching my hand forward, I was afraid to take the paper. The sound of the bell above the door interrupted, and Jarod walked in, his bag of tools in one hand as he waved a hello with the other. The smile he greeted me with turned to concern, and I realized my expression was off. I needed to get Suzette's husband out of the diner. I needed to get him out of this part of town, and send word to her to not come here. I took the flyer from his hands.

"I'll keep an eye out for her, Mr. Wilkerson. In fact, I think we can put this in the window, if that is okay with you." He nodded a thank you, and began to pay for the coffee. He was leaving, and my insides yawned a sigh of relief.

"I'm sorry, but I didn't catch your name?"

"Oh, it's Gabby. I'm Gabby. See, right here on my name tag – Gabby." I answered in a tumble of nervous words. Any measure of concern for his missing wife was gone. He huffed a short breath and narrowed his eyes in a stare.

"No! I mean I didn't get your last name. Gabby. And I don't think I gave you my last name. Did I?" I shook my head no.

"You know my wife, Suzette, and I'm going to ask that you tell me where she is." My heart sank, and I felt sick. How stupid was I? How very stupid – but I never got to answer. Suzette's husband lurched over the counter, and grabbed hold of my arm just below my hand. The flyer in my fingers closed tighter on the paper as he pressed his fingers into my skin. I reeled back and watched his fingertips grow white as he squeezed some more. Sharp pain bolted through my arm, and I winced when he pulled me toward him.

"Where is Suzette? She is *my* wife, and belongs at home. Nobody in her family knows anything. None of them have heard from her – not for weeks. I've been searching for weeks! She belongs with me, at home!" His eyes were full of anger. And the blue in them seemed more like ice. His stare took all of my strength as he pulled me closer to him. My feet began to slip beneath me as he pulled and squeezed some more.

"I, I don't know where she is!" I screamed, and tried to take my arm back. But he was too strong. Too big. He had all the leverage he needed, and pulled my arm down onto the counter, bending it until I let out another scream. Ms. Potts was up from her crossword, and Jarod was racing over to the counter.

"Hey, what are you doing? Let her go!" Jarod hollered, and grabbed hold of the enormous hand squeezing my arm. He pulled just once, and then was sent flying when Suzette's husband let go of me with a fast swing. He swung his arm, and I heard the meaty sound of the back of his hand connecting with Jarod's face. Jarod's shoes skipped and chirped across the floor, yelping as his feet scuttled in a tip-toe dance before he landed on his back. A solid thud was followed by wheezing breaths as the air rushed out of Jarod. Ms. Potts was at the side of Suzette's husband, pushing and pulling on his suit coat. He moved to face her, and began to laugh a baleful and fiendish sound, while raising his arms to block her swings.

"Whoa – whoa. Okay, just a small disagreement. I'm leaving," he laughed, and stood up from the counter. Standing across from me, I didn't feel afraid of him. Not anymore. I felt disgusted and angry, and wanted to throw a pot of coffee into his face. I wanted to see the glass break into long shards, and then use them to scoop out his luring blue eyes, leaving him blind to bump into things the rest of his life.

Adrenaline was flooding my insides, and my legs began to shake uncontrollably. I grabbed the counter to steady myself, and jumped when Suzette's husband pounded his closed hand on top of the blue flyer. His fist landed on Suzette's creased face, enticing the anger in me. For a moment, I really did think I was going to pull a pot of coffee and hurl it at his head. I thought, if he left his fist on her face for a few seconds more, I would do it.

"You tell her she needs to be home. She is my wife, and belongs at home!" He yelled, and then walked to stand over Jarod. Still lying on the ground, Jarod blinked his blank eyes with sudden activity as his legs twitched a few times. When his legs twitched again, Suzette's husband started to laugh. Jarod had been knocked out. His face was bloodied, and his nose was flattened and pushed to one side. My heart broke for him, and I wanted to cry. Not now, I told myself, and I struggled to push it back down. But my eyes began to sting with tears. Jarod looked small and hurt, lying there on the floor. He blinked his eyes again and tried to get up, but fell back. Suzette's husband laughed some more, and tapped at Jarod's leg with his foot.

"Dude – one punch? People are going to start calling you *One Punch*," he roared until he saw Clark standing next to him. He motioned with his hands that he was done. No more trouble, not today.

"I'm leaving," he told Clark, and threw a couple of twenty dollar bills on top of Jarod's chest. "For your troubles," he said evenly in a cold voice, and then he left the diner.

Ms. Potts and I were at Jarod's side, trying to help him sit up. My heart felt warm when the teenagers knelt down next to us and offered their hands to help us.

"Ewww, your arm," Brown cringed, and pointed to my arm. A set of flower petals swelled where Suzette's husband grabbed my arm. Four red marks were puffy and already showing dark purple bruising around the edges. I turned over my arm to find the fifth flower petal. I was mad. Mad for what happened, for what he'd done to us, but mostly for knowing what he'd done to Suzette. I pushed the anger down; Jarod was hurting and needed help. He gasped and choked a mouthful of blood. His nose was grossly misshapen and surely broken.

"I've got my car, I can drive him to the hospital," Jimmy offered. Brown's face lit up with a 'my hero' expression in her eyes, as she gave Jimmy a long look.

"Need to get him up," I told the kids. Jimmy nodded, and reached around Jarod's back.

"Dude needs a hospital," Jimmy muttered, while pushing up.

"No. Got my own car. Will find my own way. I'm fine. Please, just help me back to my feet," Jarod shouted in a blood-soaked voice, and then shrugged his shoulders away from our hands. I was confused. I didn't understand his reaction. He was mad, too. But he was mad at all of us. Ms. Potts reached over and held my hand, passing me a look, and then helped pull me up as Jarod got to his feet and grabbed his things. He looked around the diner, spilling blood down his shirt and onto the floor. For a moment, we all thought he'd fall over and pass out. When he was steady again, and solid on his feet, he gave a small wave to nobody in particular, and exited the diner in a near run.

"What the hell is wrong? Should we follow him?" I asked Ms. Potts.

"Did you see that? Dude went down in one punch!" I heard Jimmy proclaim excitedly as he and Brown walked back to their booth. And then I understood. Before Ms. Potts said anything, I understood, and my heart hurt for Jarod some more.

"Gabby, it's his pride. Face will heal fine, I hope, but his pride got beat down in front of you. He come over to help, and that man put him down." Ms. Potts' voice faded as she picked up the flyer from the counter. She pushed her glasses up, and said, "We gotta get to Suzette. We gotta get to her soon."

13

Sleep. It is like our own personal time travel, but a forward direction only – never backward. When I got home that evening, I only closed my eyes for a minute. I told myself, just a minute, and then a shower and some food, and then to bed. A blink was all I remember. I saw my ceiling one second, and then it was the next day. Time travel.

Ms. Potts and I stopped at Suzette's room after leaving the diner. It was near four in the morning, but I knew she wouldn't care. Having become an honorary employee of Angela's Diner, most of the time she was on our schedule, anyway. While Suzette didn't care much about the time, Mrs. Quigly a door away did care. Rushing her apartment door open, she entered the narrow hall, where a glowing dome in the ceiling cast down a yellow light. Just enough light showed us the figure of an old woman, her robe half open, wearing slippers with little dog ears and a pair of eyes looking up at us. She coughed out a midnight holler for us to keep it down, and we slunk a step back from her with apologies. Suzette apologized, too, and the three of us stood there in a stand-off, as we waited for Mrs. Quigly to go back into her room.

Suzette asked us why we were there. Was something wrong, and was everyone okay? She asked with half a smile, and I could tell she was still up and just glad to have the company. Ms. Potts did her best to explain what happened, and I did my best to apologize for screwing up. I told her I wasn't thinking. I remember holding my arm as I explained the mess I'd brought to her. The flower petals on my arm were swollen and bruised, and ached enough that I could feel my heart beating in them. When Suzette saw the bruises on my arm, she began to cry. She told me how sorry she was that he'd hurt me, and that this was all her fault. Ms. Potts shook her head, and explained as she'd done before.

"You can't wrestle that kind of mean away. It's down deep, and is a part of him. Always will be – no reforming a man like that."

We left Suzette's room twenty minutes later. She had plenty of food, and even picked up a small television using some of the store-credit from the pawn shop. Ms. Potts said the safest thing to do was for her to wait a few days. Wait him out. Reluctant eyes followed us to her door. She shook her head in disagreement more than a few times, but then finally nodded an okay. The eyes from the kitty-cat clock on the wall seemed to follow us to the door. I joked about it as Suzette repeated that it made her room look homey. Ms. Potts snorted a laugh, and said that I was right – the clock was creepy, especially the eyes. We all laughed a little at that, and then heard Ms. Quigly banging against the wall, yelling to keep it down.

I think Ms. Quigly must have been standing at her wall, waiting to hear a rustle of sound so that she had something to yell about. Suzette rolled her eyes, and we walked a soft step down the hall past Ms. Quigly's door. Ms. Potts thumped one foot down just loud enough to raise more words from behind the door. When Ms. Potts turned to me, and said that the dogs must be barking, I lost it. In my mind, I saw the doggy slippers, their upturned eyes, barking up a storm, and couldn't contain myself. Laughing helped, but I was tired and scared for Suzette. I was scared for all of us.

The diner was quiet the next day, very quiet, and I welcomed it. The imprint of a few quarters in my waist apron had me wanting some more tables. Not a lot, just a couple. When the bell rang out, I looked up to see Suzette. My eyes went wide, and, right away, I thought that when Ms. Potts saw her, Suzette was going to get an earful. She approached the counter and took to her favorite seat. She grinned a bubbly smile, and asked for coffee.

"What are you doing here? Did you hear nothing we said earlier?" I tried to scold her, but my smile got in the way. I wanted the company.

"Uh, excuse me – shouldn't you be home?" Ms. Potts chastised from behind me. The corner of Suzette's smile fell flat, and she answered,

"I know this is going to sound odd, but I think I'm safer here. With you guys and Clark. James is a coward. Always was."

"D-Dunno about that, Miss Suzette. He l-looked willing yesterday. But, you sit and stay. I g-got you," Clark expressed from behind his grill, and winked, nodding his head with confidence. I could see Ms. Potts shaking her head, but then stall as she considered what was said. She pushed her glasses up, and fixed a smile on Suzette, before saying,

"You good company, anyway. We'll keep you," she smirked, and then went to wrapping linens and silverware.

"Time to lean, it's time to clean," Mr. Thurmon announced as he exited from the back. His leg dragged a little, but not as bad as I'd seen before. Jarod followed him, a pen and paper in his hand, trying to write down what Mr. Thurmon was saying. Mr. Thurmon stopped and turned around. He put his hands on Jarod's shoulders.

"Are you sure you are okay? I mean, all this can wait a week or two – no rush, son... none at all."

Jarod held pensive eyes, and kept his attention to writing all the details down. When he stopped writing, I saw embarrassment, maybe some shame and fear, as he glanced around at us. He looked at me for a second, but then pushed his eyes back to Mr. Thurmon. Jarod wore white tape across the bridge of his nose, covering a jutting bump and a split in his skin from where the doctors straightened the bone. The skin around his eyes were blackish-blue and swollen, pooching out in a hang of heavy bags. His one eye was nearly full of broken blood vessels, leaving most of it a red wonder. Knots in my stomach had me reaching to rub the flower petals on my arm. I reached for Suzette's arm to get her attention, but she was already a step away from Jarod, and tapping on his shoulder. Jarod looked at her, a half-smile forming as the red in his eye grew glassy, causing him to wince.

"I just wanted to apologize for the trouble yesterday. I am so sorry for my husband's behavior..." Suzette tried to finish, but began to tear up. I'd hoped Suzette's words would help Jarod feel better, but he looked worse. Sweat was beading up on his face as his eyes moved around. Attention, any attention, was probably the last thing he wanted. I told myself to stay behind the counter, but was already walking over to him. Regardless of what happened, he'd come to my side to help.

"Jarod, thank you for helping me yesterday. I thought it was one of the bravest things anyone has ever done for me." His eyes lifted, and, for a moment, he saw me the way he'd seen me before, and I felt hope. Jarod pushed a smile, goofy, but good. I leaned in and kissed his cheek, and told thanked him again.

"Oh, Gabby, I almost forgot," Mr. Thurmon started to say. From his pocket, he pulled a small white square piece of paper. "Got a phone call for you – an out of state call," he continued, and slowly spun the paper in his fingers as he squinted his eyes. Trying to read his pencil scratches, he finally said, "Ahhh, here it is. Ummm... well wait, got no name, just that he was looking for *Donut*."

I never saw Mr. Thurmon crumble the paper and throw it away. I never saw Suzette grabbing at my arm as I stepped back. I never saw Jarod reaching out as the air in the room became hot and poisonous and flipped my stomach and spun the room. I reached for the counter behind me, and sat at the stool, and studied the floor while the light green tiles turned and twisted. I hadn't heard that name in almost ten years.

Ms. Potts assured Mr. Thurmon and Jarod that I'd

be okay. They left soon after I fell back onto the counter and rested on a stool. Suzette stood behind me as Ms. Potts pressed a glass of water in my hand. The glass felt cold and wet, and I wanted to throw it on my face. Instead, I pressed the glass to my cheek, and counted in my head as I breathed deeply. I would be okay, and I told them that more than a few times.

"What is the name Donut? What does it mean?" I heard Suzette ask me. Ms. Potts joined a second later, commenting on the same. Memory bubbles surfaced once more, and erupted in a stream of images. All of it was fresh in my mind, as if it were just yesterday and not ten years ago.

"It's what my father calls me. Or, what he used to call me, a long time ago," I whispered, and drank half the water.

"Donut?" Ms. Potts asked, a genuine curiosity in her eyes. A small front of offense warmed in me, and I answered,

"Yeah... Donut. What's wrong with that?"

"No, dear, nothing wrong with – just ain't heard it before."

"Well, you wouldn't, my Daddy made it up," I told them proudly. But then images and memories flooded my head again, and before I could stop it, I was crying. The memories were too vivid, and the feelings that came with them, too painful. Suzette walked around to stand with Ms. Potts.

"What is it?"

"My Daddy made that name up for me. Donut is a pet name. I was a little girl, and we went to watch how donuts were made. We even got to eat some. I remember how they tasted, they were hot, and melted on your tongue. I was so little then. My Daddy had to carry me on his shoulders because I was afraid to step on this raised metal floor. He didn't mind though, and we walked along this long window, and we could see inside the donut room. A big machine was moving the donuts, and I asked my Daddy, where did the donut holes go? He started to laugh, and I thought he was going to drop me. He joked with me that maybe the donut holes were taken, stolen, and that we needed to go find them. So that is what we did. We went home and searched for the donut holes. I didn't know what to look for, but I looked, anyway, because he was looking, and it made him smile. We had fun with it for a while, but finally I stopped looking. But my Daddy kept calling me Donut. And the name stuck. And then everyone started calling me Donut. When I grew up, everyone called me Gabby, and my Daddy was the only one left who ever called me Donut. I liked that. No, I loved it."

Ms. Potts and Suzette laughed as I told them the story. I even giggled along, remembering being little and racing around the house searching with my Daddy. And then I started to cry again. Heat pushed up from inside of me, and I tried to stop it, but then I was sobbing, and I realized you can't stop something after ten years. You can't turn it off once it starts. Suzette rubbed my back while Ms. Potts did what my momma would've done: she picked up my hand, held it, and told me to let it out.

"Spill it all," she said, and kissed my hand, then brought it next to her heart and cried with me. She said she'd try to take the pain if she could, but they weren't her tears to shed, so she did the next best thing, and held me.

I only cried for a few minutes. No roads to get on before the sun comes up. No running from me in the next hour. I let myself cry, and I let my friends help me. And, thankfully, Angela's Diner stayed empty – couldn't imagine someone coming in and seeing the three of us huddled at the counter like we were.

"Gabby. What happened? What you running from?" I moved behind the counter, and fixed some coffee. Seemed necessary, considering how drained I felt. Suzette and Ms. Potts joined in. And I began to tell them. I told them why I left Texas. Why I left my family, and, at one point, why I made the decision to never see them again.

I woke up in my bed that morning, wrapped in my

favorite comforter. Sunlight fingers squeezed through my window and tickled my eyes. Five more minutes, I just wanted five more minutes of sleep, but I had to do something that day, and the thought of it pulled me from my bed.

"Morning, Donut. Your momma left earlier," my Daddy said, and handed me a few boxes of cereal.

"What's your combination this morning?" I asked him, and watched as he studied his bowl.

"I think I've got some raisin something or other, and Sugar Smacks. Good stuff." He playfully wiped a drop of milk from his chin. "What are you having?"

I studied the cereal boxes in front of me, and picked two of them. I looked over the selection again, and picked a third. We didn't eat cereal like everyone else. *That would just be boring*, my Daddy liked to say. And he was right. So, we mixed up different combinations every morning.

"Gonna go with these three." I held them up. He gave them a look, and then a thumbs up, as he dove back into his bowl.

"Listen, I have some things to do this morning before lunch, so I won't be in the office for a little while in case you need to reach me, okay?"

"Sure. What things?" I was curious – he wasn't the type to skip a day, or even a morning, of work. He stood up from the table, and reached his hand out to me.

"Don't you worry. Gotta run – give me a hug." When I stood up to hug him, I noticed his shoes. They were different colors. Identical shoes, but different colors. He had a black shoe on one foot, and on the other, he was wearing a burgundy shoe. I started to laugh. An odd thing about my Daddy: he always wore matching shoes and belts and eye-glasses. It was just his thing – and I loved that about him. As for the identical shoes? He didn't like shoe shopping, couldn't stand it. So, whenever he found a pair of shoes he liked, he'd buy two pairs, one for each color. But never brown, he hated brown. I loved that about him, too.

"Daddy," I teased, and pointed to his feet, "you mixed up your shoes." He lifted a foot to take a closer look, and let out a breathy laugh.

"You know, what, I'm not even going to change. Let's see just how many people notice my shoes. Let's see if anyone notices them at all," he laughed again, and kissed me.

That was the last time I ever laughed with my father. The plans that day weighed on my shoulders and tore at my insides. With the house empty, I called Tommy. Tommy Grudin was more than just my first kiss. He was my first love. We were sixteen, in love, and pregnant. When I told him I was pregnant, he didn't run like I thought he would. He didn't scream or yell, or tell me I was ruining his life. He just held me, and asked me what

I wanted him to do. I loved him for that. I loved him so much. When I heard his voice on the phone, I told Tommy that I was going to be late for school, and that I'd see him after lunch. He asked if I was okay, and I told him I was fine, just that I was feeling a little sick.

An older girl, Jessica, who lived up the street, told me what to do. She used to babysit me, and, one day, while walking by our house, she found me sitting in the front yard, crying. I was just sixteen. I had my entire life ahead of me. I loved kids, but I wasn't ready to be a mom. Jessica told me about a place that I could go to. She told me that it was simple. She said that all I had to do was go in and, after a few minutes, it would be over. All done. No more baby.

When I told her that Tommy knew about the baby, she said that was simple, too. Tell him that it was a mistake. That I was wrong about being pregnant. That I was just late, and that I got my period, anyway.

It sounded so simple. The words were easy to hear: I didn't have to be pregnant, and that made sense to me. I couldn't handle trying to think about my next twenty years. But I *could* handle thinking that I didn't have to be pregnant. Jessica told me I didn't need an appointment, or a doctor's note, or anything, just that I needed to go with money and have someone to drive me. This last part got me crying again. I couldn't tell Tommy what I was considering. And there was no way I could tell my parents. I couldn't tell them. My old babysitter put her hand on mine, and I remember thinking how soft it felt, how calm and reassuring.

Jessica drove me that morning. The sun that pushed light into my eyes earlier was now tucked away behind some clouds for a nap. I was so nervous and scared, and remember shivering. I was jealous of the sun, and wanted to join in the cloudy nap. I wanted the time travel sleep again. A quick blink, and it'd be over. But it doesn't always work out that way. When we pulled up to the building, the nerves that had me shivering stretched and turned my stomach, and I lost my cereal as I got out of her car. Some Cheerios, Apple Jacks, and a kind of Shredded Wheat puddled on the asphalt while Jessica held my hair back and told me it would be okay. I think I was supposed to hold off on eating anything, anyway. So losing my cereal was fine with me.

The room was bright, but cold. Too cold. Jessica waited outside while I changed, and then held my hand as I pushed on my feet to get up on the table. The sound of paper crinkled under me as the shivering in me started again. Metal and plastic legs stuck out from the sides of the table, reminding me of a half-dead spider. They told me to place my legs in the stirrups, and I giggled at the sound of the word. I think I giggled more because of what they had given me, but then I stopped when I heard the sound of a machine come on.

The low mechanical rumble and the chatter of voices started to ache in my ears. Jessica rubbed my arm, and I heard her tell me again that it would be okay. And then all I could think about were these baby chickens. We were just kids when Tommy and I were in a class together, and they assigned us an egg. It was our job to take care of the egg. We had to make sure it stayed under a lamp and stayed warm, and had to turn the egg every day. And we did it. We did it together. We took care of the egg. And then one morning, it began to hatch.

I remember watching the egg when it moved. The shell had a smooth texture to it, and Tommy told me to put my finger on the egg. He guided my hand.

"Gently," he said, and we touched the shell. I felt a thump from inside. The baby moved. We laughed, excited by what we were seeing. When the baby chick started breaking through the shell, we cheered the little thing on until it was free. We cheered together. Tommy and I had a baby chick, and the first thing it saw in this world was our faces. I remember wanting to cry. He smiled, and wiped my cheek, and said he thought the tears were sweet and kind, and I remembered loving him that day. And I think I never stopped loving him.

I put my hand on my belly, and knew I couldn't do it. I couldn't go through with it. I didn't know what would happen to me and Tommy, and I didn't know who we would become, but I knew this was his baby, too. I started waving my hands, and told the nurses and the doctor no. I told them that I made a mistake, and that I wanted to keep my baby. I screamed at them when a nurse tried to put oxygen on me, and again when she told me to settle down. She held my arm and told me that I only needed to relax and wait. Just wait, and it would soon be over.

Jessica yelled at me to look at her. She said, "Look at me, and tell me what you want." I screamed through the mask on my face that I wanted to have my baby – that I wanted to have Tommy's baby. She nodded and said something to the nurses and doctors, and they all helped me off the table. My knees buckled, and the doctor caught my arm and gave me and Jessica instructions. He said that I should be okay, and that he hadn't started the procedure. I held onto Jessica's shoulders as she helped dress me. By the time I reached the doors, my mind was clearing, and I knew my decision to keep our baby was the right one.

When we opened the door, the outside rushed over me, and I breathed it in. But then something red and wet and clumpy exploded at our feet. We both jumped back with a scream, uncertain of what it was. Some of the remains had splashed up on our shirts and faces, and left runny red streaks across the front of us. The smell of rotting food was immediate. The explosion was a handful of spoiled tomatoes with scabs of white fuzz and blackened skin.

Remains of the tomatoes were everywhere as we tried stepping over them. Men and woman were screaming, and holding large signs with words printed in bold lettering. A sea of white and orange and turquoise poster boards danced up and down in front of us. The posters were carried on sticks, dancing back and forth with a steady low chant and an occasional scream directed at us. We grabbed for each other. I could feel the anger coming from the people in front of us. Words stood out on the posters scribbled in black marker. I could read awful, terrible things, like "Baby Killer" and "Save the Unborn from Murderers."

Another explosion of tomatoes landed in front of us, and I saw fear striking Jessica's eyes. The confidence and the all-knowing expression that helped me get to the clinic disappeared as she mouthed a curse. The crowd of protestors chanted "Baby Killer" and bounced the posters up and down. The chanting was deafening, and Jessica yelled in my ear to hurry up. We huddled together, arm in arm, and made our way into the swarm of protestors.

She yelled in my ear again, telling me to keep my head down, and to just follow the lines in the pavement. She said the protestors would move as we pushed forward, and that they wouldn't hurt us. But they did hurt us. I felt the first jab in my back, and turned to see an older man whose beard hung loose above his shirt collar. Long hairs waved around in the breeze, as he shouted,

"Bitch – Baby Killer," and then spat at my feet while pulling back the end of his sign. Another jab of a signpost hit Jessica, and she wheezed a cough out and then barely choked that we needed to move faster.

I kept my eyes on the lines in the pavement. We moved toward our car. It was slow, but we were moving. Another jab hit my side as I watched the legs and feet in front of us part to the left and right. I remember starting to scream, and Jessica held me tighter. The "*Baby Killer, Baby Killer*" chant grew to a roar, and the smell of rotting food lingered from the tomato bomb we wore on our clothes. At one point, Jessica decided to yell back, and grabbed a protestor's sign when they lunged for a strike on my leg.

"You Baby Killer!" they shouted at her.

"What the fuck is wrong with you people? You don't know us! You don't know why we're here," she screamed back at them, and threw the sign to the ground. I hung onto her arm and winced when a heavier jab pierced the skin of my leg. My knees started to feel weak, and a hot wave of nausea choked my breath as the sedative wore away. I had to stop, but only for a second. Jessica pulled on my arm, and we pushed forward.

"Baby Killer, Baby Killer," echoed in my ears, and a sudden urge to cry hurt more than the sign posts. I glanced at the sky, trying to pull the tears in, the sun was still napping, and I wished I could hide up in the clouds with it. When I looked over the sea of colored posters, as they continued to bump up and down, another fear came to me. What if they were moving with us? What if they formed a circle around us and were walking all the way to Jessica's car? Jessica yelled for me to put my head down. And I did, but not before someone grabbed a fistful of my hair and pulled it out of my head. Screaming, I put my head down and followed the lines in the pavement.

The legs and feet continued to part ways and move to the sides of us. Relief began to settle in place of the nausea. The "baby killer, baby killer" chanting was softer. I could hear my own breathing, and realized I was crying, after all. We were passing the worst of the crowd. The remaining protestors continued to move around us, but then a pair of shoes stood in front of me. They didn't move. A black shoe, and a burgundy shoe. And then I heard my Daddy's voice.

"Donut?" My heart sank, and all I could do was look up into his face. His eyes were filled with confusion as he shook his head back and forth like the poster boards' dance.

It was a moment we shared, a terrible moment, and it ended who we were. "Daddy," I cried, and reached for him. He extended his hand, just enough to touch the paper and plastic medical bracelet the nurse had put on my wrist earlier. The confusion drained from his face. Deep lines emerged above his eyes, and his face turned red like the tomato remains on our clothes. He raged and cried and screamed at the sky, and pushed my hands away.

"But, Daddy," I pleaded with him, reaching my hands to him, and again he pushed me away.

"I don't know you. My God... Gabby, how could you consider *this?*" He sobbed. "I don't know who you are – I can't know a person that could do *this*! Who could do *this* to an innocent life?"

He stepped back into the pack of protestors, and screamed their chant.

"But, Daddy," I cried out to him, stretching my arms to reach him, "I didn't do..." and a hit came from my other side, and it was deep and under my ribs, and stole my breath. I gripped Jessica's arm, and thought I was going to black out, but the stars that raced in front of my eyes rose up to the clouds.

By the time I could see clearly enough again, my Daddy was walking away from us and holding his face in hands. "Daddy!" I screamed after him. "Please, Daddy!" I screamed some more. But he only shook his head and kept walking.

My heart ached. My heart broke! I wanted my Daddy, I needed my Daddy, and he turned away from me. Jessica got me to my home later that afternoon, and then wished me luck as I got out of her car. When I went to my room, it wasn't my room anymore. It wasn't my home. How could I face my Daddy? How could I face my momma, or anyone? I wasn't thinking, not at all. A voice in my head said to run, get on the road, and run.

My dog sat on my bed, his eyes were big, and his ears were pressed flat against his head. He whimpered, and I believe he knew there was something off, something wrong. Dogs know. Sitting next to him, he nuzzled my arm, as if trying to ask what happened. I wiped the silliness away from my eyes, and kissed him on the snout, and told him I had to leave. He whimpered some more, and nuzzled my chin. I kissed him again, and kept the tears in my eyes.

Run, I heard in my head, and poured the books out of my school backpack. My life as a teenager ended, and any evidence of it was dumped out onto my bed and remained there. For all I know, it may still be there. I raced around the house and gathered a few pieces of clothes, another pair of shoes, and whatever cash I could find. That is all I had with me. And that is all I left with. From the road, I looked back once to see my dog watching me through the window. I cried for the first mile, but then wiped that silliness away, too.

Ms. Potts and Suzette never interrupted. They never

asked a question, or passed a look to one another. I didn't remember seeing Clark come from around from the grill, but there he stood, a cup of coffee in his hands, and his eyes on me.

"Gabby, that is horrible..." Suzette started to say, and then an awful thought rushed though me, and it scared me. What would they think of me now? What would they think about what I did, or planned to do? A crash of feelings filled with pain and fear and sadness hit me, and I shook.

"Please, please don't judge me," was all I could get out before Ms. Potts pulled me into her arms.

"Shhhh, ain't nobody here gonna judge anyone. That ain't our place to do. You done nothing wrong in my eyes. What was done to you is unspeakable," she finished. I passed a look to each of them.

"G-Gabby, your family – we love you," Clark added.

Suzette leaned in when my eyes reached hers, and asked, "Gabby, but what about the baby?"

Images of Tommy and the baby chick raced across my eyes, only to be replaced by memories of a dank and musty motel room and a filthy bathtub.

"I lost the baby a few days later," I said, and pushed back another wave of hurt. "The first cramps started the next morning. I had coin-sized bruises on my legs and around my back and my front," I started, and circled my finger and thumb to show where the bruises landed.

"They were a deep color, just sickening bruises. The protestors left their marks on me that morning, and, by that afternoon, I was losing my baby."

I could only tell them some of what happened next. The images were still in my mind, and I suppose they would be the rest of my life. The cramping didn't pass. Instead, a burning started inside of me. That is when I considered that my baby and I might be in trouble. My skin felt warm, and, with the blankets pulled away, I laid on my side and prayed for the pain to stop. I told myself it was nothing. I told myself it was stress, and that the cramping was normal. I prayed that my baby would be okay. My skin got warmer and sweaty, and I began to feel cold. That's when the vomiting started. Something was wrong.

So much pain came then, and it was from deep inside. It was a pain like I'd never felt before. I prayed, and cried through some of it. I didn't know if my baby would stay alive. I didn't know if I could stay alive. I kept praying. Praying that we would be okay. I remember sitting on the floor against the bed, cold beads of sweat under my eyes and above my lip. I remember holding my belly and talking to my baby, and saying to hold on, to please hold on. But when I felt the wet between my legs, I knew it was blood, although I hoped it was sweat. I remembered hearing about bleeding in early pregnancy, and that everything could be okay. I prayed harder.

A hot twist of pain pulled me to the floor of the room, and I remember digging my fingers into the carpet and clutching fistfuls of shag, trying not to scream. But I did scream – pain pushed me on my knees and elbows with fistfuls of carpet as a run of sweat dripped from my nose. I felt lightning spasms inside, pulling me apart and holding me on the floor of that motel room. At some point, I blacked out for a few minutes. No time travel this time. When the room was in my eyes again, the spasms were worse, and a heavier flow started. I grabbed a towel and held it under me, and then started to shake. My baby was leaving me.

By the time it was dark outside, I had to lie down in the bathtub. I held the towel between my legs and waited to die. It was a white bathtub, but dirty and old, and it had a drain that was caked in black mildew. But I didn't care, I couldn't save my baby. I remember pushing my fingers along cracks in the lip of bathtub and into some of the holes where porcelain used to be. I remember waiting as the sweat ran down my face and the blood spilled out of me. The tub felt cold under my skin, and my teeth chattered. The pain that pulled my insides didn't stop, it didn't get better. A few times, I thought I'd pass out again. I wanted to call out for someone. I wanted them to get my parents, to get Tommy. But then I felt my baby leave me, and I shut my eyes and prayed that I would keep bleeding. That I'd bleed until there was nothing left of me.

There was a familiar pain in the eyes of Ms. Potts and Suzette. They knew this pain; they'd been where I'd been. It wasn't the same, but, then again, it was. I didn't realize it before, but we shared something, a loss. I felt closer to them for it. Looking at their faces, I wondered if there was something bigger than us, greater than us. Something that had brought the three of us together. Could there be? I'd like to think that maybe there was.

"But I didn't die in the tub. I cried when it was over. I lost our baby. I don't know if I was going to lose our baby anyway, or if the visit to the clinic was what caused me to miscarry. But I couldn't go back. It wasn't just my Daddy – I could never face Tommy again. And I think maybe I might have killed Tommy, too."

Suzette pulled her hand to her mouth after I mentioned Tommy. She considered what I said, and I'd considered it more than a few hundred times since seeing his parents. If we had our baby, would Tommy have joined the Army after college? If we had our baby, would he have even gone to college? A blend of questions haunted me after hearing about his death. I didn't dare explore more, or speculate what might have been if the decision I made had been different. One decision, a decision I made on a breezy afternoon while sitting in my yard changed our lives forever.

14

Some days at the diner start out busy, and then stay busy. Today was one of those days. The bell above the door, ringing every couple of minutes, had me lifting my chin to see who was coming and going. Sounds of our busy diner played back a tune of dishes and dinnerware, and people talking and laughing. I loved that sound, and would never tire of hearing it. As for my feet, I wish I could say the same, but that was a different story. Like Mrs. Quigly's doggy slippers, my feet were barking. I kept a steady pace of back and forth to pick up plates of food from Clark, and was certain a rut of footprints, just my shoe size, were fixing a path from the booths to the counter, and to the grill.

Even Mr. Thurmon was pitching in to help where he could. He'd donned a waist apron to clear and setup the counter when bussing was needed. I liked having his company, but found that I was keeping an eye on him, hoping he was okay, while trying to keep an eye on everything else. He struggled through his pain, but was surprisingly quick in working the counter; he'd obviously done this a few times, maybe even a few thousand times. It especially helped having him with us when he chased out a few campers who'd held onto one of our booths for more than an hour. Just kids having fun, but not ordering anything, they cursed him some, and he scoffed a laugh as he told them to please come again. The counter was busy that night, and we wouldn't have been able to manage the floor without him.

While you might think the counter would be the easier section to work in a diner, it wasn't. Not at Angela's. Quite a few of our regulars were singles, meaning they were here for a meal, and then out the door. No socializing; no need to. So, the counter not only saw more faces, they were inclined to move fast, very fast. When Mr. Thurmon's neck started to pink up, I knew he was already beginning to tire. Soon after, the pink crept into his cheeks and darkened to a near purple, and, at times, his leg seemed to drag behind him like a dead limb. When he caught himself falling into the counter's edge, I told him he should take a break. He was working into his second hour, and looked as though it had been a full day. He knew it, too. The stumble in his step and the cramping in his hands fought him constantly. A few times, I saw him try to shake out the dysfunction in his fingers, as though conjuring a spell to rid himself of the disease. Whatever relief there was to have remained fleeting as his expression soon turned to disappointment and sadness when he looked at his hands.

When a plate smashed to the floor, and the diner hushed in a momentary lull, I could tell he was ready to take a break. The pain was too much. Red-faced with sweat over his eyes and above his lips, he gave me a smile and shrugged. I told him that I'd take care of the broken dish, but that the cost was coming out of his pay. He laughed, but his voice sounded tiny, and I could tell he was embarrassed. I also thanked him and asked if he'd like to take a few minutes and let me get him something to eat or drink. He hesitated when he reached to pick up a piece of the dish, but then stopped altogether and pulled himself up. He grabbed a cup of coffee, and took to the empty seat he was clearing before the dish crashed at his feet.

"Buyers are coming today. Probably would be better if I stay more professional-looking, anyway," he conceded, and blotted the sweat from his brow.

"Buyers?" I asked, thinking my voice sounded naive and unknowing. Of course, we all knew about the pending sale – the detective had made certain of it. Hearing the words aloud stung a bit. Regardless of the danger to Ms. Potts and Clark, selling Angela's still felt wrong.

Mr. Thurmon lifted his eyebrows with a warm expression, and maybe some relief, which I suppose was at the prospect of selling. "Buyers... from the neighborhood. They own a few buildings, and want our plot to expand one of their businesses. 'Strategic' they called it. I didn't think this place would sell... didn't expect it would *ever* sell. And never considered the dirt we're sitting on was worth more than the diner," he finished, his expression absent of any reservations, or remorse that I expected to see.

I loved Angela's, and the thought of it being torn down hurt inside. As I watched Mr. Thurmon drink his coffee, I felt angry. I felt mad that he could just sell Angela's, only to see it torn down. Destroyed. It wasn't my place to think anything, and I couldn't imagine what he must be going through, but I was angry. Putting his cup down, Mr. Thurmon smiled and winked at me. I gushed a little, and any resentment I held onto disappeared. I felt sad for him: sad that he didn't feel an attachment to his mother's place like I did. He may have, but just didn't show it. Not now, anyway. I'd like to think that was the reason.

"Well, if that'll make you happy, then I suppose that is the best thing for Angela's, isn't it?" I shot back, and realized my voice sounded short and gruff. Sometimes my voice doesn't catch up with my mind. I refreshed his cup and then told him I had a table waiting. Guilt pressed on my shoulders as I walked away. Maybe four or five steps, and regret told me to go back to him and apologize, but Mr. Thurmon was already up from the counter. He was moving to the front to greet two Asian gentlemen dressed in dark suits – the sound of the bell rang out as the door closed behind them. One of the men wore a cream-colored tie, which matched his brown eyes, while the other wore a tie with spots, which clashed against the stripes on his suit. Neither of the men was smiling. Mr. Thurmon shook their hands with vigor, and made a polite enough smile, waving his arm in a half circle, napkin still in hand, to show off the inside of the diner. Ms. Potts took a notice of the men, too, only her concern was more pressing. She glanced to Clark, and then to me. This was real. This could happen. The diner could be sold and torn down.

"Can we get some fries and milkshakes?" the table in front of me asked. The teenage girls from the all-girls school were back for a visit, sitting in their pre-assigned seated locations. Funny how people do that. Staring up at me with freckles and dimples, a set of braces, and even a little acne, were the familiar faces of Blonde, Black, Red, and Brown. I assumed from the chatter and banter that they were all friends again. Brown's companion from the other day was notably absent, and I wasn't about to bring up that little sunburn lie. *Let them stay friends for at least ten minutes*. A small giggle pressed behind my lips.

"So, no to the coffees?" I directed toward Blonde in a sarcastic tone. The three other girls turned to Blonde, wide eyed.

A whisper of "really?" came from one, while another answered,

"I know, right?" I tried not to laugh, but Blonde smirked, and then giggled herself, and answered,

"No, no coffee today. Some french fries and milkshakes. I think three chocolates and one vanilla, right? Oh, and an extra straw." The other girls nodded, with Red waving that the extra straw was for her. I remembered. A minute later, and they were engrossed in teenage talk, their time with me completed. Brown kept her head up long enough to catch my eyes, and, when I saw her, she motioned to my arm where the flower petals had changed colors and wilted some. I grinned a thank you for the concern, and she dove back into the chattering amongst her friends.

Milkshakes and fries, a deadly combination. Add some ketchup, and you're hitting upon a true local delicacy; the *locals* being the girls at my table, that is. By the time the milkshakes and fries were served to them, *Keep on Truckin´* had joined me at the counter, as did one Detective Ramiz. Clark kept his eyes on the grill, and Ms. Potts tended to the booths in her section. And I am sure she left one eye working the tables, while the other stayed on the detective. The air felt electric again; it felt uncomfortable. Thankfully, it wasn't as heavy as before.

Twenty minutes into a second serving for *Keep on Truckin´,* and another plate of fries for the girls, the detective stayed seated at the counter, his coffee steamy and black, having ordered nothing more. No manila envelope came from across the counter. No accusations. No commentary. No questions.

In my head, I heard my father's voice calling out *Donut.* It was his voice from the day I'd seen him at the clinic. And it was the last time I'd heard him call me by that name. I heard his voice again. Until now, I assumed Tommy's parents must have contacted my Daddy and Momma. How else would they know where I was, or that I was a waitress in Philadelphia, and at Angela's Diner? But with the detective across from me, would he have called? Could he have called them? The last thing he said during a recent visit was: *Call your parents – children should be civil to their parents.*

"Thoughts got your mind twisted up, do they?" Detective Ramiz blurted over the counter. His voice cut through my contemplation, and I flinched.

"How so?"

"I can see you're up in your head about something. Want to share it? Maybe something I can help you out with? Maybe these two, here, you're working with told you a little something you need to share with me?" he answered, and sucked down more of his coffee. *Keep on Truckin´* gave the detective an odd look, and then turned back to me. I realized *Keep on Truckin´* hadn't seen the detective before. He didn't know who this man was, or why he would be making propositions. I nodded to *Keep on Truckin´*. I appreciated him looking out for me.

"Call your parents yet?" the detective continued, and motioned for more coffee.

"Why? Why do you care if I call my parents, or not?" I remarked, and shook my head, annoyed.

"Children should be civil to their parents is all. Not a matter of respect or disrespect. Just civil, like you're being with me right now. Civil," he answered, exposing his round nubby teeth in a pretend smile. "I'm trying to finish my job with this last open case, and, in doing so, your friends, here, are going to be affected. Yet, *you* can be civil, can't you?" When he finished, I poured the coffee and didn't say a word. He had a point.

Memories of my parents came to my mind. I saw images go by, like flipping through an old photo book. From birthday parties, to learning how to ride a bike. And then I saw my father walking away from me, his hands pressing against his head, as people with signs poked at me with wooden posts, throwing rotting tomatoes at me while screaming. I could feel tears swelling my eyes, and I pulled a needed breath. If only they knew... if only they knew that they may have been the ones who killed my baby.

"Parents need to be civil, too," was all I could think to say, and moved on to pour *Keep on Truckin´* more coffee.

"Gabby, you gonna be okay?" *Keep on Truckin´* asked, a piece of food dancing from the tip of his mustache as his lips moved.

"Thanks, I'll be fine," I rushed out, and swiped at one of the tears that got away.

"How we doing back there, Clark? Getting all your cooking in before you go back to prison?" Detective Ramiz yelled. The diner went quiet as people sought out the source of the loud words. I watched heads turning, their wandering eyes furrowed by concern. Mr. Thurmon and the potential buyers of Angela's were standing outside. I didn't realize till then: the buyers had no reason to look inside. They were tearing down Angela's. They hadn't heard Detective Ramiz. None of them looked through the glass into the diner.

"A man belongs in prison when he's done a thing like what you've done. I'm getting close, you know. Very close. Not long, now..." Detective Ramiz pulled a napkin over his mouth and pushed out a phlegmy cough, "... not long now, at all."

"S-Sir, why don't you just leave? J-Just leave," Clark stammered.

"Now, now – look who has a voice, all of a sudden. All this time, I'd thought prison had got your tongue," the detective shot back, smiling. I hated that smile. He looked around the diner, and then back to Clark. "I heard in prison, they knock your teeth out – if you're prone to biting while on your knees, that is. But never heard of them taking your tongue. Ain't that right? Guess you best get ready for more of the same!" Detective Ramiz laughed, and finished his coffee. Ms. Potts approached, and stood next to the detective. Her face was fixed in a scowl, anger thinned her eyes, and she pressed her lips until there was just a thin line above her chin.

"I know you think you have business with us, but you don't. We trying to work here, and, as you can see, we full. Now, I suggest you finish up and leave, or order yourself somethin' more than coffee. You're wasting a seat at the counter." The detective raised his hands, and waited until Ms. Potts took a breath.

"Oh, but Ms. Potts, I don't think I have business, I *know* I have business. Look out that window," he started, and pointed toward the front. "Who do you think those men are? They are bringing a wrecking ball with them, and they are going to destroy this place. And when they do, I'll be here to see it happen. I'll be here to see what is under that floor, over there, where Clark is standing. Ain't that right, Mister Clark?" Detective Ramiz yelled some more, taunting the cook.

"Sir, you got someplace else to be?" *Keep on Truckin´* interrupted. While he asked the question, his tone was more of a demand, telling the detective that he should listen and leave. *Keep on Truckin´* stood up next to Ms. Potts, towering over the detective.

"Got some fine people, here. I don't much appreciate anyone messing with their business. And, mister, from where I'm standing, you're messing with their business." Detective Ramiz's smile grew into a sneer, as he moved his eyes to *Keep on Truckin´*. His smile was long, with the corners of his mouth pulling back heavy lines of skin below his eyes. He looked like an evil clown, smiling, and enjoying the challenge from *Keep on Truckin´*. The detective pulled his badge from his hip, and held it out just long enough for most in the diner to recognize it before tucking it away to hang from the front of his belt.

"You might want to sit your trashy ass back down. As part of serving the law, seems my business is wherever I need it to be." *Keep on Truckin´* gave the badge a once over with his eyes, as a smile peeked out from beneath his mustache.

"That's fine. Just remember, if you didn't have that badge, we'd have ourselves more to talk about," he finished, and took to his seat. *Keep on Truckin´* stayed on the edge of his stool, close to Ms. Potts. His expression stayed bright and wanting, while he kept his eyes fixed on Detective Ramiz. The detective's grin went flat, and I could see he took to the truck driver's words. Ms. Potts forced a straight face, but I could see she was trying not to laugh. The strain of the moment lifted, and I gave *Keep on Truckin´* a warm thank you with my eyes.

"Good boy," Detective Ramiz praised sarcastically, and then added, "Badge works, but, given the time and purely coincidence I *assure* you, I do have to run. Clark and Ms. Potts, I'll be seeing you." And, as Detective Ramiz left the diner, I watched as he pulled up one of our napkins and cupped his mouth. As the door closed, I could hear a burst of coughing and choking, and saw Mr. Thurmon and the potential buyers of the diner turn a concerned eye. For them, the detective was just an old man struggling to breathe. But to Clark and Ms. Potts, he held their future in a manila folder.

Keep on Truckin´ looked a little agitated from the rush of adrenaline, but shrugged it off with a snicker. I thanked him for stepping up like he did. Ms. Potts patted his back with gratitude of her own, and tended to her tables.

"On the house," I started. "Name the slice of pie you want. All fresh and homemade," I added.

"Homemade!" he scoffed, "You get them from the Food Mart up the road, and then charge three times over cost. Who you fooling? I recognize the boxes."

"Shhhh... how about two slices?" *Keep on Truckin´* giggled, and winked his eye. "How about one of them rhubarbs, there, and an apple? Thanks, Gabby. Oh, and whip, lots of whip. Love that whip." I nodded and returned the smile.

I fixed *Keep on Truckin´* his slices of pie, and then fixed a slice of rhubarb for Clark. It was his favorite, and I'm sure he needed it. When I went back to hand it to him, he was gone. When I went to his cot, I saw that his book was gone, too. Clark had run.

15

It was official: Suzette had joined our family at Angela's Diner. Three days had passed since that night when Clark grabbed his book and left the diner. Where he went to, we didn't know. Where he lived, we didn't know. Nobody knew anything about Clark outside of the diner. Even Ms. Potts had to shrug her shoulders when Mr. Thurmon pressed for some answers. I'd begun to suspect that Clark may have lived here, in the diner, all this time. He had a cot to sleep on, he had plenty of food to eat, and he had his book to read. And when he needed to shower, there was the city's YMCA, where nobody asked your name. It was just a small walk two blocks over and one block up. He could easily have visited the Y while Ms. Potts and I were busy with crosswords and word searches. I suspect that Clark was living at Angela's and standing guard, watching over their secret that he and Ms. Potts had buried twenty years earlier. I suppose, in a way, he might have considered this his penance for killing the husband of Ms. Potts. What would the penance have been for Mr. Louis Elmore Potts if he'd killed our Ms. Potts? This was Clark's burden to bear, and if that meant living in Angela's Diner, then that was what he was going to do.

For now, all we did know was that Clark was gone. I missed him already, and felt afraid for him. Ms. Potts kept her feelings close to her heart, and my prying only got me a sentence or two, followed by a waggle of her finger while she choked back her concerns. I could tell she hurt with Clark not being with us, but something told me he was okay; I'd like to think that he was, anyway. While Ms. Potts wouldn't say it, I wondered if she thought he was okay, too. Clark could stay gone. Stay hidden. Just disappear, like I had. After all, how much time could Detective Ramiz have? The detective looked worse with every visit to the diner. The color of his skin was fading to a light gray, while his breath grew shallower and wheezed more loudly. He was running out of time. And he knew it, too – he knew there was a race between his own demise, and the demise of Angela's Diner.

Mr. Thurmon was in a bind – he was all knotted up. He kept worrying about who he could get to take Clark's place behind the grill. No cook and a near full diner can make for a hectic afternoon service. Being short-handed couldn't happen at a worse time. The misfortunes of the fast-food restaurant, the one that had been draining away our customers since opening, left us with a full diner for my shift.

A sudden flood of faces had made Angela's Diner the hot spot after school again. Some included new faces, while others were old. And then there were my personal favorite faces: the teenagers. The crowds kept us busy well into the evenings. And all it took were a few roaches, a couple of mouse droppings, and the sightings of a mammoth rat named Bertha: I'd learned the name from the teens. Bertha was an overweight tame and docile thing that may very well have been someone's pet once. My guess was that Bertha had escaped her owner, or maybe had been let go to fend for herself. In her travels, she found the back of the fast food place and started feeding on fast-food scraps from the trash. The teens told us the rat was bigger than some of the city rats they'd seen around the trains, but that it was tame, and did little more than wander around outside the dumpsters, its big belly hanging from the middle and dragging on the ground.

Once the sightings inside began, everyone laid a claim to seeing Bertha. First, it was a run under the tables and over shoes and the tops of sandaled feet. Then it was a run across the tables, where some even said a

French fry was hanging from Bertha's mouth. I dismissed that last claim, but laughed as the teens told the story. Eventually, Bertha was trapped and taken away, but not before the damage was done.

In all, the sightings of Bertha did wonders for our small diner. We watched the story unfold from Clark's TV. It was an eager, tell-all news-story by an ambitious reporter standing in front of the fast-food restaurant. With long blond hair, she was a pretty girl wearing square glasses and trying to look more studious than she was. She told the story of the rat that ran through the dining area, and of the food inspector's visit that followed.

We laughed watching the little television. It wasn't just the misfortunes of the restaurant that had us going. It was the kids huddled up behind the reporter, some with *Free Bertha* posters. The news-story was live, and they must have known it. All at once, they lined up and yanked their pants down, drawers and all, shooting a moon into the camera. We could hear one of the kids yelling, "Kiss my Bertha!" The camera man started to laugh, and the screen jostled up and down while the reporter, her blond hair blowing in front of her eyes, yelled into the microphone. And then the screen went black for a second, maybe more, before returning to the anchor desk. The anchors were laughing, too.

How long the fast-food restaurant would be closed

to the public was a mystery. What it meant for Angela's Diner was a springtime run of full booths and busy counters every day, every hour. I wouldn't say it out loud, but I liked it. I liked the rush of people, and the sounds of the dishes clanking, and the constant smell of food. It made my heart feel good. It reminded me of those first moments when I walked through the door and saw Ms. Potts and her big glasses and blue hair.

As for her, she worked the grill in place of Clark, but did so with much reluctance. She hated working the grill, and made sure to complain about it every chance she got. And when Mr. Thurmon was in earshot, she expressed her dissatisfaction even louder. When it was quiet, and there was a moment for us to get off of our feet, she said nothing. Not even a smile. And sometimes I'd hear the sound of crying coming from the back, where Clark would normally be sitting in front of his TV. Later, she told me that she cried for the trouble she'd brought to him. She cried for the trouble that was to come. Mostly, however, she cried because Clark was missing. He'd picked up and disappeared. And, sure as rain was falling during our April afternoons, the detective would find Clark, even if we couldn't.

While Ms. Potts worked the grill, I waited the tables and the counter. Mr. Thurmon continued to help, and thankfully he did know what to do. But his arthritis kept him slow, and he struggled to keep up. Our regulars didn't mind, though. More than a few times, I'd see them get up and help themselves around the counter with an appreciative smile from Mr. Thurmon. They'd even clear a plate or two for him, and set up linen and silverware after a quick wipe of the towel hanging from Mr. Thurmon's shoulder. But a few were rude, and sometimes they were mean. Under their breath, they'd call him names. Who does that? And for what purpose? He'd chuckle a feeble apology, and offer them ten percent off their bill, or a free piece of pie.

After a few days, I could see how the hours wore on Mr. Thurmon. And then the time came when he just couldn't spend another day away from his law offices. With a glum look and a shake of his head, he told us we had no choice, but we'd have to shut down during the afternoon rush; at least until another waitress or cook could be hired. Only one waitress and one cook was too much to ask of anyone.

"What if I work the counter?" Suzette beamed, and immediately ran around the counter to survey her idea. Mr. Thurmon wiped at the sweat over his eyes, and flexed the pain out of his hand as he watched Suzette race around him. He stood, quiet, as she glanced over the shelves behind her and under the counter, and rested her hands on the register. Her eyes glinted light from outside, adding a sparkle to the excitement in her step.

"I can work the counter – me and Gabby!" she

hurried with an enthusiastic grin. Mr. Thurmon raised his eyebrows, and nodded a shy grin to her idea before turning to Ms. Potts for her approval.

The image of a magazine cover entering Angela's Diner that one night crossed my mind. I saw Suzette dressed in her emerald green evening gown, ample cleavage teasing all the eyes within reach of her. I also saw her wearing a waist apron and taking an order from *Keep on Truckin´*, the corners of his bushy mustache jogging up and down. The images playing back in my mind made me laugh aloud, which caught Suzette's attention. It caught everyone's attention. An uncomfortable spotlight made up of collected curious eyes was on me. Suzette stopped her survey behind the counter. A hurt look in her eyes squashed the enthusiasm that was waiting for an answer from Mr. Thurmon. She frowned, and pushed her shoulders back to face me.

"What? What, you don't think I can do this?" she spat, and then looked to Ms. Potts for some support. Ms. Potts raised her hands and shook her head with eyes wide, trying to hold back a smile.

"Girl, don't look at me. I didn't say anything – might be good idea though, I like it. Might be a great one... heck, hunny, you always here with us, anyway," Ms. Potts finished, and punched her hips with her clenched hands.

The eyes were back on me. I had to say it. I had to say something. The laugh was innocent enough, but my timing was terrible, and it showed on Suzette's face.

"I think it would be an excellent idea. And I'm sorry if I giggled at the wrong time." Suzette's expression lifted, as a smile crept to the corners of her mouth. She batted her eyelids, and I wondered if I had really hurt her feelings.

"So, what was funny... if it's okay to ask?"

"I just think Mr. Thurmon should maybe consider charging an extra quarter per cup of coffee with you serving them – just add a little shake," I answered, and shook my chest with a quick jiggle. I know it was lame, but considering her history with her green evening gown, I went with something less memorable.

The spotlight of eyes moved off of me when Suzette laughed, and joked, "As long as I don't have to flash a boob!" We all laughed a little harder at that, and Ms. Potts' eyes grew, her glasses falling to the end of her nose.

"Well, mind you, please," she started, "I sure ain't jiggling or flashing nothing. Might hurt someone, or break a dish when my pups hit the counter!" she yelled over us, lifting her breasts in each hand. And we all broke out in a laugh that was loud and filled the diner.

Even Mr. Thurmon gave in with a hearty fit of giggling. Though he tried to stifle the fit with a raise of his hand, he finally joined in until his face turned shades of purple with tears streaming down his round cheeks.

When the laughs faded to a whimper, Suzette returned to her survey behind the counter.

"So, can I have the job? Like Ms. Potts said, I'm always here, anyway. I can work the counter, and Gabby can work the floor." Mr. Thurmon raised his brow to each of us, looking for an objection. When none was to be had, he extended his hand to Suzette, and welcomed her as part of the family. Suzette pulled his hand in with an eager tug, and moved around the register to hug every bit of him.

"Okay, okay – just a job, no reason to get too worked up. Might find yourself hating it by the end of the night," he joked, but with some sincerity in his words.

"Might not have a job for too much longer, anyway – ain't that right?" The lightness of the moment dimmed as Suzette pulled away from Mr. Thurmon. Ms. Potts stood again with her fists on her hips, stern eyes fixed on Mr. Thurmon.

"Junior, how long before the suits buy our diner and tear her down? Why you want to let that happen?" she asked, and I realized it wasn't just about the body in the floor behind her. Angela's was her home, and it had been Mr. Thurmon's, as well, for most of his life. Mr. Thurmon pushed one foot and then his other, and fell back onto the stool. He pressed his hand over the counter, and rubbed the top of it as his lip trembled.

"This is hard. So hard. But I can't be the owner,

anymore. I can't keep my family and my law practice, and be the owner of my mother's restaurant."

"What if we run it – you know, you own it, and we run it?" I pushed in. He gave me a grateful glance, and then answered, "Because, I'd *still* be the owner. When the next *Clark* leaves and we can't staff a shift behind the grill, then I'd be back behind the counter. When the next shipment from a supplier fails on a delivery, then I'd be back on the phone, asking what happened. Once you're an owner, you're always involved."

"But what if we kept that part of Angela's out of your hands? Why not let us do that for you?" He considered what I said. For a second, I thought he would give the one line proposal some serious thought, but he didn't.

"I understand, Gabby, but it is easier this way. No responsibilities; I can just walk away." And I could see and hear the relief in his words as he said that.

"What about us, Junior? We's family," Ms. Potts jutted in, and then pulled a hand to her mouth. Mr. Thurmon's face changed like it had before. In front of us, we saw Junior, young and innocent and sweet. His eyes filled and emptied as he got up and embraced Ms. Potts. The two hugged for a minute, consoling each other. When he pulled back, he was still Junior, and he walked back behind the counter, surveying like Suzette had eagerly done earlier.

"Don't you think this is hard for me? I mean, I look

over there at the front window with my mother's name on it, and I remember that day. I remember her standing outside in the sun, full of life, and healthy, and her eyes gleaming with pride as they finished the last of the lettering. And then I look at the coffee machines, and I remember her installing them *herself*! Or the toasters over there, and her coming back from a supply house, grinning ear to ear about how she'd saved a few dollars. And this counter, and the cut in the corner from when we had to replace the cash register. The men installing it dropped the old one, and my mother got so angry that her beautiful counter wasn't like new anymore. It wasn't perfect. This isn't just about the diner – I see my mother in every part of what Angela's is." Mr. Thurmon stopped, and shook out the pain settling in his hands.

"Junior, I..." Mr. Thurmon's face was his again, the little boy was gone. He held up his hand, and added, "I'm sorry, Ms. Potts, I truly am. If there were other options, if someone else bought the diner to keep it running, then Angela's would stay. Nobody called about the diner. Not one. In fact, the only call was for the plot. It broke my heart. It did. But with the fast-food place up the street, I guess nobody wants to own a diner."

We said nothing. The four of us stood for what felt like a long time, and then Ms. Potts walked over to Junior, and hugged him again. She put on a smile, and slapped his cheeks between her hands.

"You live, Junior, get on, now, and you live. I understand. Ain't no need to explain yourself – never to me. I overstepped, and shouldn't have. Always gonna love you, and always gonna have a place in my heart just for you."

Junior nodded as Ms. Potts spoke to him. I could imagine him as a little boy with Ms. Potts telling him a wise tale, or teaching him something new and exciting. He nodded, and choked back a tear-soaked breath. When I saw that their eyes were wet, it made me want to cry. And I did. I looked at Suzette, and saw her swipe her cheek. A few minutes later, Mr. Thurmon left the diner in our hands for the remainder of the shift.

I helped get Suzette started behind the counter, while Ms. Potts went back to the grill. And our timing was good, as the bell echoed an arrival, and a young couple sat down at the counter. No better time like the present. I stepped back and let Suzette take the order.

She took to them easily enough, offering her smile, and placing menus in front of them. The woman looked pregnant, but I wasn't certain until I saw her cradle her belly with her hand. She dropped her chin, a smile brightened her face as she stared somewhere far away, while rubbing her hand over her belly.

Suzette lifted the coffee pot, and the gentleman nodded eagerly, while the woman said that a glass of water would be fine. The rings on their fingers confirmed that they were married. Suzette gave me an elated smile, and I raised an approving eye, confident that she could handle this. When the woman pulled up a small white paper from her pocket, her eyes darted to her husband, and she threw the paper in his face. Shaking a fist at him, the woman began to yell, as Suzette stepped back, confused. The man stood up, pointed his finger, and jabbed at the air as he spouted brief rebuttals to whatever his wife was yelling at him. After another exchange, the man grabbed his coat and stomped out of the diner. The woman pressed her face into her hands and began to cry.

"What happened? What was that?" Suzette asked, tugging at my shirt. I was so drawn in by the story unfolding, that I didn't see Suzette approach me. She hit one on her first customer. I was working the diner at least a month before I hit my first one. Ms. Potts was stretching her neck from behind the grill, eager to learn more of the story.

"An order of coffee and tears," I mumbled. Suzette pinched her eye, and asked,

"I've heard you and Ms. Potts say that before – Why?" Suzette asked as Ms. Potts walked around to stand with us.

"Well, now that you're working here, there's something you should know. The three-to-three shift sees a lot of people, and we hear a lot of stories. And, sometimes, those stories come with tears. They're not here for the food, just a cup of coffee, and a place away from anywhere. A place where they can sit and let it out, whatever it might be. And, as waitresses, naturally, we get to hear the stories."

"An order of coffee and tears," Suzette acknowledged, then added, "I don't know if I should be angry or embarrassed. Or both." I put my hands on her arms, and turned her to face me.

"You never have to feel anything but comfortable with us. Okay?" Suzette bit her lower lip, and mumbled a shy agreement.

"You two go on and help the poor woman out. Looks like she needs some ears to hang her words on. Looks like it'll be a good story," Ms. Potts instructed.

"An order of coffee and tears," Suzette said smiling.

16

A good story can always get the feet moving, Ms. Potts told me once. And I never forgot it. I told the same to Suzette as I followed her to the counter, where a young, pregnant woman sat, crying. A white piece of paper, the one that had chased her husband away, lay on the counter, isolated and seemingly innocent. But it was hiding a dangerous secret that threatened a revelation if touched. Sitting half folded and wrinkled, the crumpled words held a power that piqued my curiosity. With her hands covering her face, I could see the wet of her tears running past her fingers. I stretched my hand with a linen cloth between my fingers, and tapped her arm lightly. My eyes stayed fixed on the paper.

She mumbled a thank you, wiped her face, and then fixed an angry stare on the paper in front of her. The woman froze. She remained like that for what seemed minutes. No movement from her. And, through the corner of my eye, I saw Suzette's head leaping back and forth. We both flinched when the slap of the napkin hit the counter top. The woman had seen enough of the crumpled note, and swatted it away from her, as if it were a dangerous wasp, readying itself to sting.

"Ma'am, are you okay? Can we get you something?" Suzette began with a sympathetic tone.

"My husband is an asshole. A *fucking* asshole," the woman spat, her eyes stuck on where the paper had been. I blinked, and I think Suzette did too. We shared a brief raise of our eyebrows. The colorful language sounded odd coming from the woman in front of us. She was young, but not that young. She wore a cloud of curly reddish-brown hair, and had a round face with pout cheeks and blue eyes which were big and glassy. She dressed up with just enough makeup to keep things simple, but elegant. A thin frame held her eye-glasses, and carried two tones of the colors chocolate and purple. I hadn't seen the style before, but immediately loved it.

"I'm so sorry – I never talk like that. I think it's all the hormones, but he *is*... he is a fucking asshole," she laughed, as her hands fell to the counter with a thump. Suzette's eyes were wider, and a smirk formed on her lips.

"So, you *are* okay?" I asked, confused, but more curious than before. She waved a hand, shooing off the tears, and set her eyes on something behind me. A guilty look played on her face as she eagerly bit at her upper lip.

"My doctor says it's okay – just one or two a day," she started, and then pointed to the coffee, "Can I get a cup... a big cup?" She asked, and I understood the guilt was one of pleasure. Suzette tended to the coffee, the smirk on her face rising in the corners. *An order of coffee and tears*, I could almost hear her saying with her eyes. A door had opened in the conversation, and I wondered if Suzette had caught it. I certainly did. I jumped at the opportunity.

"Ma'am... doctors? Everything alright?" I asked, while Suzette brought over some creamer and sugar. The woman touched her belly, and her eyes beamed with the same look I'd seen earlier.

"Yes, everything is fine. I'm pregnant," she answered quickly, and wrapped both of her hands around her middle. After a pause, she turned her attention to the counter. Bringing the cup of coffee to her mouth, she pulled in the whispery steam with her first sip. Delight reigned on her face, and she closed her eyes.

"Mmmmmm – that does taste good." The bell over the door echoed, and pulled my eyes. Jarod entered the diner, tools in one hand, clipboard in the other. Was it Thursday already? Had we been so busy that I'd lost track of the days?

Dark bruising remained under his eyes. The worst of

223

it, though, had passed, leaving behind patchy green-yellow, with fringes of blue and purple. He'd taken all of the white medical tape off of his face, and I wondered if it was more out of a sticky or itchy annoyance. The fracture on the bridge of his nose had scabbed over, leaving behind an ink-black lump that stood up high on his face. I hoped it would heal cleanly, and that the inky break on his skin wouldn't scar. I hoped that every time he looked in the mirror, the ragged mark wouldn't remind him of that day; the day when Suzette's husband chewed up his dignity, and vomited it in a single back-handed swing of his fist.

My hand was up in the air before I realized it. I pushed a smile on my face, though, admittedly, there was little effort needed. I wanted Jarod to see me like he had before. I didn't want any misgivings, or see him shy away out of embarrassment. Coming to my side that day was brave – braver than anything anyone had ever done for me.

Images of my Daddy flashed in my mind. Images of him pulling back his hands as I reached out for him and called to him. The jolt of a painful memory stabbed me, and I reached down where, years before, a sign post was pushed into my belly. The memory hurt. After ten years, it still hurt. I suppose it always would.

But Jarod came to my side that day. When Suzette's husband held me down, Jarod defended me. No questions or reservations. Just bravery. Jarod wouldn't see it like that, though. How could he? He was hurt and ashamed. And I wondered what must have been going through his mind when he opened his eyes; the sheer confusion of it all.

I felt a heaviness, a knot in my belly. How awful for him. How terrible. My heart quickened a beat, and filled with a sensation that sparked another memory of something I'd felt before. Angst shuddered more emotion, and, at that moment, I knew. I knew what I was feeling was real. It wasn't just something my mind had grown from a seed planted by Ms. Potts' words. I felt something for Jarod.

My eyes felt moist as the realization of feeling something touched me. It touched me deep inside, where a decade ago I'd left a hole open in my heart. The hole remained there like an old dried well, sitting in a field, and spelling danger to anyone who'd dare set foot near the edge. But now, a finger of hope's simple touch warmed me. Filling the hole, the emotion of it all overwhelmed me, and I had to take hold of the counter, uncertain if I was going to laugh or cry. Looking at my feet, I wasn't running. In my heart, I wasn't sad. I think I might've been happy.

"Psssst," I heard from behind me. Ms. Potts waved her hand toward Jarod. I gave an abrupt nod, telling her I knew he was there, and saw him looking at me. His eyes looked beautiful. I offered him a sweet smile as he passed me along the way to the back. I mentioned I'd fix him something to eat when he was done, and he told me he'd like that. Suzette stood, transfixed by the two stories playing out at the same time. She listened to the woman. Claire was her name, and she watched the exchange between me and Jarod.

"My husband's been cheating on me. And I think it's been going on for some time," Claire revealed. She spoke it plainly and directly, and passed a look to both of us. She lifted her eyes and gasped, "Finally, I said it! The words have been racing in my head, but now I said it." I stepped in, and put a hand on hers.

"Did that have something to do with that piece of paper?" Suzette asked. It was a good question: she wanted more of the story. Claire patted the top of my hand, and lifted her coffee cup toward me. Jokingly, I told her I'd give her one more, but wouldn't be held responsible for any more after that.

"Two years. That is how long William and I worked to get pregnant. We thought it would be so easy. All of our friends started a few years ago, and we felt it, too. We felt it was time... time to start our own family. We planned it all, from the cradle and the room, to a bigger house and colleges. Planning was fun... I loved it. But it didn't happen like it did for our friends. We couldn't get pregnant." She stopped, and sipped at her coffee. The same delicious expression showed in a grin with relief and a contented smile.

"I could drink that all day," she started to say, and then dropped her eyes to her middle, laying a hand on her belly, "But not for you. Only two cups, and no more. Have to keep you healthy," she added with a baby-talk tone in her voice.

"Two years is a long time. But it happened?" I offered.

"It did. It happened. We have our miracle. It wasn't easy. So many times we almost gave up – but our doctor was certain it could happen. And it did." She settled her eyes on her coffee, and I could see she was tearing up.

"I'm not sure when it started, but when I smelled perfume on him the first time, I asked about it. He said something about a drive to a meeting with an associate. And then there was the receipt – it was a lunch meeting, he told me. But for *two,* and with *wine,* I asked him? And then he told me the fertility drugs were making me think things that weren't real. He said that I was connecting disparate points in time to make up a story. I hated that he said that – who says that? I hated that he made me think that he was right. And that piece of paper... it's a note with an address. I should go over there. I should confront the bitch."

"But how can you know for sure?" Suzette asked, and refreshed her cup with just a few drops to keep it tasty hot. Clair motioned to her coffee cup, pinching two fingers, she whispered,

"Please?" Suzette put on a reluctant smile, but then added a couple more drops.

"I wasn't really sure, at all. Not at first, but then I found the piece of paper. It was on the floor of his car, on the passenger's side, and I grabbed it on our way over here. When we sat down, I asked him about it. He didn't try to deny anything. I almost wished he had, though. He said a few things, but then ran. A guilty man runs – they always will," she answered, and the tone of her voice went soft, almost quiet.

When I heard the words "a guilty man runs," my thoughts went to Clark and his book. I thought of his list, the one that kept his life on a piece of paper – it spelled out who he once was, what he'd done, and who he was today. I thought of the man in prison who gave him his book. And then I thought I might know where Clark was.

That was the last I heard of Claire's story, and the last I thought about Clark and where he might have gone. When the bell above the door rang out, bright afternoon light and a hot breeze pushed into the diner. An older man stood at the door, his silhouette keeping his features hidden from us. We were back into the throes of the spring season's summer-warm days, and the figure at the door held his jacket over his arm, as though he'd been walking a while. The bell rang again, as the door closed behind him. I've made a habit of giving a brief look to those that enter, and then immediately a quick check of the booths, their linen and silverware, and the counter. We were between the rush of late afternoon lunches and the dinner crowd. It was quiet for the time being. If he was alone, he could sit at the counter.

There was something familiar about the man, and my eyes went back to him. When his eyes found mine, he stepped forward, and the air in my lungs became hot like the outside breeze, and I coughed it out. I wanted to run. Run to the back where Clark had been, and then run out the door. It was my father.

"Donut?"

"Oh, sweet Jesus," Ms. Potts said from the grill. I heard the sound of metal on metal when she dropped her spatula. She was around to the counter and by my side a moment later, holding my arm.

"Gabby, girl, it'll be fine," she started to say, but I couldn't hear more than the whisper of her words. My eyes were stuck on my Daddy. He was old. So old. The thick black hair I shared with him was almost all gray, and the perfect skin on his face was a mass of lines around his eyes and cheeks. He looked more than just old, he looked tired.

"Gabby. Please," he pleaded, raising his hand, and took another step into the diner. Images of him pushing my hands away came to mind once again, and I shook my head.

"I don't want you here!" I yelled. He stopped abruptly, and shuffled back a step, as though he'd bumped into a glass wall he couldn't see.

"I'll sit," he started, and motioned a hand toward a booth, "I'll just sit, and... and I'll order something. Can I do that?" Ms. Potts let my arm go, and, without a word, she brought two cups over to the table nearest my Daddy, and poured coffee into each. The diner was so quiet. I kept my eyes on my Daddy, and listened to the sound of the coffee pouring.

Ms. Potts looked up at me once as she poured, but said nothing. She didn't ask. She didn't seek out an objection. Nothing. Two cups – she took two cups, and poured the coffee. Not a word. But that said everything to me. When she was done, she glanced back at me and motioned with her eyes to the booth.

I shrugged at him, and saw in his eyes the man I remembered when I was a little girl. They were the same eyes that held me after a tumble while learning to ride a two-wheeler. They were the same eyes that told me I'd be okay, and planted a kiss atop my head after a nightmare. It was my Daddy, and, for a moment, the pain and anger fell away. I moved to the booth, and Ms. Potts followed with an arm on mine. I heard her say again that it'd be okay... that I just needed to sit and listen.

My Daddy was seated by then, stirring creamer into

his coffee. His eyes stayed on mine. I sat down across from him, and, at once, felt old. I wanted to be nine again. I wanted to be running to him and crying after having scraped my knee in a fall. But I couldn't do that. Ten years had passed, and never once did I consider my age. Inside, I still felt like a teenager, the one who learned her way across the country.

Seeing my Daddy was like looking into a mirror. The reflection showed me that I was no longer the teenager who had run from home. I wasn't walking the blacktop of sleeping roads while the sun struggled to stretch an arm over the mountains. I wasn't *that* Gabby anymore. I wasn't Donut.

"What do you want?" The words just spilled out of my mouth. It was all I could think to ask. He cupped his hands around his coffee, and placed it on the table.

"Look at you, Donut, look at how grown up you are," he said in a lilting Texas accent. The sound of his voice and the sound of home in his words touched my heart with a guttural volley of emotions. My tongue had lost the sound of Texas some time ago during my journeys across the country. It may have been the travels on the back roads of Colorado, or the rain-soaked walks in Seattle. And, like everything else from Texas, I buried the memory of it.

"What do you want?" I repeated, and then scolded, "My name is Gabby! Just Gabby!" He winced when I said that. But could he have expected anything different? Should he have expected anything different? In my heart, Donut died in a motel room ten years earlier. I buried Donut and my baby, and the bloodied motel towels. I buried them in a field behind the motel, five miles north of the Texas border. The winds whipped tall grasses around my body while I cried and dug with my fingers. I clawed at the hard dirt and stone until the hole was deep enough, and then put the towels in the ground. I remember staring into the hole, staring at the towels and the blood. Donut laid in the ground, too, and I covered them up. I stayed on the ground next to them until the fading stars and reaching sunlight told me it was time to go; to leave this place and never come back. I told myself that Donut died so she could watch over my baby. She stayed there, and I never saw her again. Fury was what I felt next, and I thought I might pick up the hot coffee from the table and throw it in his face.

"I hated you. Did you know that?" I yelled, and didn't care if the few in the diner heard me. My Daddy winced again, and raised his fingers to try to say something. I wouldn't listen. I couldn't listen. He put his hand down and said nothing. Words tripped on my tongue as I tried to say something mean and hateful. Rage stole my voice. Thousands of confused words raced around my head. They felt like hurtful bees, stinging my mind and feeding on my fury, spewing sour honey.

"Gabby, I am so sorry. I see that day at the demonstration in my head all the time, and wish I could do it over again. I wish I could have acted like your father, and not like that man you saw. I'm not that man anymore; haven't been since the day you disappeared." He explained, but then his expression changed. "Where did you go? How could you disappear? We thought you – " he stopped to catch a shaky breath. "Your momma and I thought you were dead. How could you let us think that? How?" More bee stings followed, and the sour honey poured into my mouth. I wanted to hurt him, but then I considered what he'd said, and thought of my momma. And then I heard Detective Ramiz's voice. *Be civil to your parents. Be civil.*

"You don't get to ask me that. You never get to ask me that!" I spat at him.

"But... but Gabby, your momma and I spent years looking. How could you let that happen?" Shock staved off the bee stings, as I realized my Daddy was angry, too. His Donut disappeared, and they thought she was dead. He might've even hated me for disappearing. But didn't I want him to think that? Did I care what he thought?

My emotions twisted into a knot, and turned my insides. I sought out the faces of my family, Ms. Potts and Suzette. Their eyes were welcoming when they found mine. Suzette blinked an "I love you" while Ms. Potts nodded, and brought us over some more coffee. She didn't say a word, just poured the coffee, and rested her hand on my shoulder before returning to the counter. The warm touch of her hand settled me and gave me strength.

"I had to leave – and I never wanted to see you or anyone from home, again."

"Your friend Jessica told us everything. We saw her days after you disappeared. She told us that you didn't go through with it. She said that you changed your mind and that the two of you were trying to leave, when..." he stopped then, and I thought it was because of my expression.

"Go ahead and finish it – say what happened next! I want to hear you say it!"

"... when you two were confronted by the demonstration," he finished in a breath that was choked and tortured.

"They killed my baby, Daddy, they did it! Did you know that, too?" I screamed at him, and the swarm of bees stung me as the pain and hate poured from my eyes. The brief stoic expression my Daddy held disappeared in that moment, as he took in the realization of what had happened.

"No, no, no," he mumbled, and shook his head. He fell apart and cried. We both cried, and, before I could stop it from happening, I reached for him. I reached for him like I did that day at the medical center, and this time he reached back. I hated myself for doing it, but I needed my Daddy. I fell into him and held him, and let myself love him.

The moment was brief, and when he was sitting across from me again, I told him, "This doesn't change anything. I left home – *had* to leave home, and won't be going back."

"Tom Grudin was looking, too," he started to say, and the image of Tommy came to mind. "He never knew about what happened."

"Is that how you found me? Tommy's parents?" I asked. A dull ache touched my heart when I saw images of Tommy and the baby chick. My father nodded, and added,

"His mother stopped in to tell us about her son and her trip to Delaware. She told us she didn't recognize you. I never knew you and Tom Grudin were close. Not a couple, anyway."

"Only one – ," I told him, then breathed, "Just once."

"I was sorry to hear he died. He was a hero, saved some lives, his mother told us."

"Did you and Momma go to the service?" I'm not sure why I asked him that, but it seemed right for one of us to be there. I felt a pang of guilt thinking about Tommy. My Daddy nodded.

"You said you *hated* me. Does that mean you don't

hate me anymore?"

I considered his question. Ten years had passed, and every day since made the next day a little easier. I told myself I stayed away because I hated him, but wondered if I stayed away because it just got easier than thinking about going back.

"I don't think I ever hated you, I hated who you were that day. But you're my Daddy..." And then I couldn't finish what I wanted to say. The emotions of it all knotted my insides until my words were gone again. He reached across the table, took my hands, and finished for me.

"Maybe we can be okay again one day. I know that isn't today, and don't know when that might be. I just couldn't live with you hating me. I love you, Gabby. You're my daughter, and there is nothing you can do that will ever change that."

At some point, I think we both realized what had happened that day at the center. What had changed who we were, who we all were, wasn't something we could make better in a conversation. After all, how do you fix, in a few words, something so terrible? I suppose the only thing he could do next was to tell me he loved me. And he did.

17

Hours disappeared, but it seemed only minutes since my Daddy left Angela's Diner. He went back to his hotel. Before leaving, he insisted that we meet for a lunch the next day, where we could talk some more. The emotional drain of seeing him and reliving some of what I'd buried took its toll. My lungs didn't want to fill – I couldn't catch my breath, and my legs and arms were heavy and clumsy. Exhaustion is a funny thing when it is in your head. It's even funnier when your brain turns to a mass of oatmeal without rhyme or reason to the thoughts being produced. That's how I felt, and no amount of coffee seemed to shake the tired out of me.

Jarod stayed around. He was a week behind on his work schedule, and decided that he would like to take me up on the quick meal I offered. I was happy he had to work late; I was happier that he worked in the back while my Daddy was here. But what I liked most was when Jarod asked if I was going to sit with him for a while. I'd brought him some coffee and a grilled cheese sandwich with fries, and, as I walked away from his table, he reached out and took my arm. I felt gentle kisses of his fingers on my skin, and then I felt them drape over my hand. My heart fluttered, and I told him I'd be right back.

"Sit, Gabby – I've got your food, and have things covered," Suzette chimed from behind the counter. She was joined by Ms. Potts, and the two of them stood, huddled up like spectators. I threw a stern glance at them, and they hurried to move like bugs in the dark when the lights come on. A moment later, and Ms. Potts was showing Suzette how to drain the ketchup bottles. Ketchup, for the most part, drains itself – all we do is stand up the bottles. The two of them continued to watch and talk the way I would have done with Ms. Potts. I tried not to laugh, but could feel my cheeks pushing up against my will.

My smile stayed; I could feel it fixed on my cheeks as I sat across from Jarod. I couldn't stop smiling, it was almost funny. Suzette brought over my sandwich and some coffee. She planted a wink of her eye, and giggled a school girl laugh before saying hello to Jarod, and asking him if there was anything else he needed.

"Just a drop more of coffee – thanks," he answered politely. I liked the sound of his voice. I know that might seem strange, but it was true. Suzette leaned in to pour his coffee. Images of her wearing the beautiful green evening gown came to mind, and that frumpy feeling found me again. I tried to push a smile, but it was forced, and I felt uncomfortable. What I saw next made my heart swell. Jarod didn't look at Suzette. He didn't look at her like the other men in the diner. When she poured his coffee, his eyes didn't fall past the opening in her shirt. When she smiled at him and walked away, his eyes didn't follow. He didn't see Suzette; not like that.

"Can I ask you something?" he said, breaking my gaze. I nodded, and he asked, "Would you want to maybe go out with me sometime? I mean, on a date, with dinner and a movie." Jarod fixed his eyes on me again, his lips pursed with an expression that was both sincere and vulnerable. I tried to swallow, but felt my heart in my throat as my skin turned warm around my neck.

"Gabby?" he asked, and his expression began to change to one of embarrassment. Had I waited too long? I was quick to raise my hand to tell him to give me a second. I'd just been asked out on a date – a real date. Grabbing for my coffee, I felt nervous and giddy at the same time.

"I'd love to," I gushed, and felt my smile stretch from ear to ear. I didn't hold it back, or push it away in an attempt to look less interested. The embarrassment that was settling on his face disappeared as he sighed

239

into a full smile.

The bell above the door sounded. Habits are habits, and the sound pulled my eyes up away from Jarod. Detective Ramiz walked in, and brought with him the smell of a cold spring night with storms resting for the evening. He shook off the remains of the day, and plodded toward a seat at the booth next to mine.

"Well, Miss Gabby, nice to see you again," Detective Ramiz began, and tilted his fedora. "And, I believe, this is Jarod – the diner's handyman. In fact, the handyman for the entire block. Sir, my name is Detective Ramiz," he ended with an outstretched hand. Jarod shook his hand, but said nothing – offering only a short nod before turning back to face me.

The glassy sound of something rolling interrupted as a ketchup bottle fell over onto the counter. Ms. Potts grabbed the bottle before it left the edge of the counter.

"You have some more business here this evening?" She asked. The detective bared his nubby teeth, and hissed a wheezy laugh before answering.

"Why do I have that reaction with people?" Whether he meant it to sound funny or not, nobody answered.

Waiting for a reply, the detective finally resigned, and took a seat in the adjoining booth. Sitting, he wheezed a few laughs into a napkin. And, as before, when he was done, he opened the linen to reveal the squashed butterfly remains of phlegm and blood. He was getting worse. Did his color look grayer since the last time I saw him? I think it might have.

"Ms. Potts, no need to fret – this visit is purely a self-serving one. I'm here for a late supper. Nothing more," he answered, and plunked the napkin in front of him, while collapsing his body to rest against the back of the booth. The detective was dying. Thoughts of the diner's secret crossed my mind, and a small feeling of hope rested in me. I shook the thoughts away, and felt guilty for thinking such things.

"Then we b-best get you a m-meal so that you can be on your way," I heard from the counter. And then I heard Ms. Potts squeal, and saw her drop everything in her hands to run to Clark. Coming in from the back, his book in his hands, Clark stood at the opening, his large frame a familiar silhouette. I could make out his smile. As I stood up, I took Jarod's hand in mine, and moved next to him. His eyes filled with surprise, and he eagerly moved so that I could sit next to him.

"Jarod, I like you. I think I've liked you for a while... just didn't know how to say it, or show it," I stammered, trying to rush my words. He raised a brow, his lips turned up in a grin, and then my hands were on his face, and I kissed him. It was a good kiss – his lips felt velvety soft and supple. I was glad I kissed him, especially when he began to kiss me back. The kiss lasted longer than I thought it would. And I loved that it did.

When I pulled away, I went back for another short peck, and then told him, "I've been wanting to kiss you for a long time. I have to go and see Clark. And, yes! Yes, I would love to go out to dinner and a movie with you," I beamed, and then ran off to the back room.

Clark settled back in behind the grill, and, while he griped about how unkempt and filthy Ms. Potts left his work area, we were just happy to hear his voice.

"Took me a small vacation," he began, and shouldered a spatula onto the metal of the grill to scrape away the remains of Ms. Potts' cooking. "Took me a p-pilgrimage, of sorts. Went to see an old friend."

"The list!" I blurted, and he stopped scraping the grill long enough to lift his chin and smile at me. He waved his spatula toward me.

"You *were* l-listening."

"I listened to all of it. Was your friend still there?" I asked, and heard the bell ring out from the front. Suzette pressed a hand on my arm, and said she'd get it. Ms. Potts seemed to hear nothing as her eyes were moist, and stayed fixed on Clark. I couldn't tell if it was anger or relief, or a combination of the two that was stewing in her eyes.

"He was there. Old n-now... very old," Clark paused, and straightened his shoulders and continued, "Ma'am...

told him I d-done something. Told him I'd done something that made me want to run. I told him I was running, and that I'd never go back, 'cause I was afraid." I heard shame in his voice. He did plan to run. He was scared, and he ran.

Ms. Potts' eyes widened, but only for a moment. "You stop any worrying. Whatever happens is gonna happen. No stopping it, now. I'm gonna tell 'em I killed my husband. Should've told the detective that a long time ago, and freed you of the burden. I'm ashamed of myself."

"It's okay, Ma'am, I think it's g-gonna be okay," Clark said to Ms. Potts, and then turned to me, and added, "Old man laughed when I told him I still had my list. He laughed c-'cause I never read it or throw it out. 'It's j-just a list. Read it, and throw it away,' he told me. When I feel the n-need, I can start over. We can always start over," Clark finished, and, as he looked at us, I saw a young man in his eyes. I knew that he would be okay, no matter what happened.

The first scream sounded like something from a movie, and the three of us lifted our eyes, uncertain of what we had heard. I heard Suzette's voice in the second scream, and my heart dropped when I realized the voice of the man screaming was her husband. My feet were clumsy and heavy again as I pushed to run to the front. Fear weighed on my legs, and I grabbed my arm where

Suzette's husband had held me down. The flower-petals had wilted and gone away, but their memory stayed deep, like the memories I'd tried to bury.

James Wilkerson stood near the center of the diner with a knife in one hand, and Suzette in the other. A spilled cup of coffee lay on the counter where Suzette liked to sit, leaving me to wonder how it was that James approached her and took hold of her. Her face was a mess of tears and steaks of blood. The blood fell over her eyes in long narrow streams, while her husband held her up by the back of her neck. Her feet dangled beneath her – the toes of her shoes skipping over the floor while she struggled to fend off the pain of being suspended.

Suzette's husband was powerful. He was stronger than anything I could imagine. I saw no evidence of struggle in his eyes as he held his wife above the floor. His powerful hands gripped tightly, his fingers wrapping around her neck, and an awful thought came to mind: he could snap her neck if he wanted to. He was much stronger than I ever thought a man could be. And I wondered how it was Suzette could have survived his attacks all these years.

The sound of Suzette's feet skipping against the floor chirped and screeched amidst the cry of another scream. James towered over Suzette, and, except for Clark, he towered over all of us. His clenched fingers glowed white as he held her up in the air, dangling like a rag doll. Dark spots of red stood out amidst broken skin on his fist, and I guessed it to be the bloody remains from Suzette's mouth, where he punched her. The side of her face was on fire with a raised lump that crested in purple marks. A tooth and pool of spit and blood puddled on the floor next to the stool. Suzette screamed again. The sound was terrifying, and I heard Ms. Potts begin to beg and plead and cry. And then I heard her praying. She prayed to Suzette's husband, as if she were in church and seeking answers to make things right.

"I said, put her down!" Detective Ramiz demanded from the booth where he stood, his hand on his revolver, sitting in the holster on his hip.

"What are you going to do, old man?" James shot back. His words were mangled and slurred. I didn't see it at first – I only saw Suzette and what was happening to her, but James had been drinking. On the floor, a bottle of whiskey lay on its side, open and dripping. The bottle had been kicked and left under a stool at the counter. The picture of what might have happened became clearer, but that didn't matter. James put the knife behind one of Suzette's ears, and pushed the blade forward. Blood sprayed onto the floor as the knife passed through the back of her ear. She screamed a murderous sound, and my heart pressed against my chest while I grabbed and pulled on Clark's arm.

"We have to do something! He's going to kill her!" I

screamed at Clark with words that fell on ears stifled by a same mix of fears. Suzette pulled at her husband's hand, and swung aimlessly with her arms as blood ran to the nape of her neck and along the front, above her chest. She wore a necklace of red like the pearls he'd once given her. Clark stepped around me to better survey what he might be able to do. James stopped immediately, the hideous smirk and laughter disappearing. He pointed his knife in Clark's direction. Clark stopped. The detective pulled out his revolver, and pointed it at James.

"Ms. Potts, Clark – I trust you've dialed 9-1-1 by now. I trust you did that, and that the patrol cars are rolling, and will be here in the next minute. Do you understand what I am trying to tell you, sir?" Detective Ramiz yelled, and then doubled over as he grabbed his mouth and choked out a fit of coughs. The detective's gun was down: it wasn't pointing at James, and James knew it, and began to laugh again. The laugh was animal. It was a jackal sound, and he clapped a foot against the floor in rhythm to his howling.

"Old man – this is a joke! Say it isn't a joke," James began, but then grew grim-faced, and put the knife's pointed edge to Suzette's eye. "This is *my* wife, and I'm going to see to it that nobody ever loves this pretty face again!" And, as he finished his words, he ran the blade under Suzette's eye just enough to open her skin. Suzette screamed again, and punched aimlessly with her hands.

She beat on his arm and hand, but he didn't move. And, as he continued to cut her skin, a pool of urine formed beneath Suzette. Her bladder let go and dripped from her shoes, and when her eyes found mine and I saw the terror in them, I started to cry and scream, and ran to her.

All the air in me disappeared in an instant, when her husband's leg bolted upward, and the bottom of his shoe met me square in my middle. I couldn't pull in enough air as silvery white streaks of stars raced in front of my eyes. The silver streaks flew around, and then were gone, and there was nothing but the blackest of black.

"Just breathe," I heard, and saw Jarod's face come into view. Ms. Potts' face was next, and both of them were helping me sit up. The jackal sound of his laughter shook my ears, and Suzette's scream singed my heart. He was going to kill her. But he was going to torture her first, if we did nothing.

"We just need to wait, Gabby, please wait. I called the police, and they assured me they are on their way," Jarod said in a quiet whisper, inches from my ear.

"One Punch, is that you? Ha! Oh, this is sweet. It is you! Come on over, One Punch. I had some fun telling everyone about you." When Jarod heard the nickname, I saw his eyes go cold, and his face long, absent of all expression. As he stood, anger rose on his cheeks, and his skin went red. He turned to face Suzette's husband. I reached to pull him back, I pushed my hand into his hand, but my fingers fell away when he let them go.

"Put her down," Jarod began, and then balled his hands into fists. "How about we finish what you started the other day?" he added, and waved an invitation. James' jackal laugh grew into a roar, and his eyes squirted tears as he watched Jarod dance a boxer's pose and continue to wave on invitation after invitation with his fists. James' hold on Suzette wavered. He roared again, and I saw Suzette's feet begin to take hold of the floor. Her foot slipped in her urine. It slipped again, but, as her husband's hold of her weakened, she took back some of her footing.

"Squads are going to be here – I suggest you put her down now!" the detective yelled. He'd regained his stand and his gun was fixed on James. Sweat poured from his face, and his gun shook and threatened to fall to the floor.

"Come on, you big fucker. Try and take me on when I'm watching. When I can see you. Just try! No more sissy back-handed shit. Come on," Jarod yelled, as James shot more tears. Suzette's feet touched a firm hold of the floor, and, in one motion, she swung her other foot and connected with her husband. She knocked the wind out of him just long enough to loosen his grip on her.

"You bitch –" he started to say. Suzette fell to the floor, where she grabbed the whiskey bottle. James turned, his hand reaching for the prize he'd lost. Suzette screamed, and threw her arms in a full swing. An explosion of glass opened the side of her husband's face. The glass rained down inside the diner, splintered shards landed on the tables and the counter and floor. Glass and blood went in every direction. James heaved a sickening moan and fell forward in a stutter of steps. His right cheek hung open from below his eye down to the line of his jaw. He fell toward Detective Ramiz in an effort to regain his balance. We heard the detective scream for James to stop, and then a flash of lightning filled the diner twice. Thunder and the smell of gunpowder came next, as James' body tumbled to the ground. Past the ringing in my ears, I could hear faint sounds of glass continuing to tumble around us, and saw Suzette's husband gasping for air. Blood spread on the floor around his face, and he gasped again, sucking in air and spitting blood. He pulled one final draw of breath, and then stopped.

"He was coming at me!" Detective Ramiz screamed, "You all saw it! He had his knife in his hand and was coming at me!" Clark stepped over to James and knelt at his side, taking care not to step in the pooling blood. He pressed two fingers to his neck. Clark looked back to us, shaking his head. Suzette's husband was dead.

"He was coming at me!" the detective screamed again. Clark stood again to face Detective Ramiz. The detective kept his gun drawn. The barrel was pointing at Clark, waving back and forth as the detective continued yelling.

"Clark!" Ms. Potts pleaded, and, at that moment, I knew what might happen. I knew what could happen. We all did, even Clark.

"He was going to kill her. And he was coming at me," the detective wheezed, as blood dripped from his mouth. He belched a cough, and more blood dripped, while he continued to hold his gun. Clark took a step toward the detective. He stepped again until the gun was just inches from his chest.

"He was going to kill her," the detective whispered.

"I know. You d-did the right thing. You did good. Nobody's going to know any different. Not ever," he told the detective, and reached his hand over the gun and put it on the table. The detective's eyes fell to James' body on the floor. He stared, his face empty. Blue lights reflected off the smoke and glass as the sound of the approaching police squads filled the diner. I ran to Suzette, where Jarod was already helping her to a stool. Like the detective, her face remained empty, and her eyes stayed fixed on the body of her husband.

"It's over," she said plainly. I brought her chin around to face me. Bloody tears ran down one side of her face, while the other remained dry. Her cheek and jaw might've been broken, and some teeth were missing from where he punched her.

"It's over," I told her, and then held her. She didn't cry. She didn't scream. Suzette stared at her dead husband's body with eyes that were far away. I held her and told her again that it would be okay.

"It's over," she repeated, and I nodded and continued to hold her until the paramedics took her away.

18

Thirty days and thirty nights had passed since Suzette's husband held her by her neck and laid a knife on her skin. Thirty. A full month. Yet, the images and sounds, and even the smell of it all seemed to linger. A lot of talk went back and forth after that night. Speculation that James Wilkerson wasn't going to murder his wife, that, instead, it was just another in a string of his abusive acts toward his wife. When the police were satisfied with their notes on the case, the folder closed, and Suzette's husband was still dead. What was never investigated or questioned were the two bullets that ended up in James Wilkerson. We all told the police the same thing. James Wilkerson went after Detective Ramiz. He had a knife in his hand, and charged the detective. And that is how we saw it. How we all saw it.

Suzette didn't come back to the diner... not right

away. It was slow at first – a day or two, and then three, and then finally she was with us all the time. The places where her husband's knife did touch her skin were still healing. Large stretches of baby pink skin replaced the black threads in the stitched wounds. She'd have the scars as a reminder forever. But the scars we could see were probably just the superficial ones – the deeper wounds would likely never heal.

Once Suzette was back to a full-time schedule, she continued to work with us. She wanted to work. We always did need a third waitress on our shift, and it was fun. Having a third waitress made things easier, especially with the fast-food joint nearly empty every night, no thanks to Bertha the rat.

Suzette poured me a cup of coffee and lifted her chin, and I told her thank you. These days, there was a peaceful look in her eyes, but there was sadness, too. I suppose the fear I'd come to expect seeing was gone. Suzette was free of feeling scared. The anxiety that sat deep inside her like a cancer had died on the floor of the diner thirty days earlier. She no longer worried when it was going to happen again, when she'd feel the angry side of her husband's hand. She wasn't looking over her shoulder, or quietly stepping through her house like a mouse going unnoticed. She didn't flinch to loud sounds, or shrink back when the front door opened. She was free of him.

"I cried, you know," she said in an even tone. A long scar ran under her eye from where the bloody tears had come from. Another scar ran down her neck from behind her ear. "I cried at James' funeral." She poured herself a cup of coffee, and leaned on her elbows so that we were closer, our faces just inches apart.

"But why? I mean, why would you cry after what he did to you? After all the things he did to you?" Suzette's eyes were watering, and she turned her head away from me, but I think I could understand it. A quiet moment passed. And when Suzette was ready, she found my eyes, and said in a broken breath, "'Cause I loved him. And I know, in my heart, he loved me. There was a side to him that I got to see – that I got to love. I just wish I got to see more of it." Suzette clinked her coffee cup against mine, and raised it in a mock cheer.

"You getting ready for a date, or something?" Ms. Potts yelled as she brought a plate of fries and milkshakes to the teenagers. Blonde, Red, and the other girls were in their usual booth, in their assigned seats. They gave me a wave, and a thumbs up. The girls spotted me at the counter, and, if not for the fact that I was talking to Suzette, they very well may have looked right past me. I was out of uniform, so to speak. I wasn't wearing anything waitress-like. Not a thread. I was a customer. That's right, a customer. Actually, I was waiting for Jarod. We had plans for a dinner and a movie. Finally.

Sitting at the counter, a warm giddy feeling stirred in my belly. Some butterflies, too, left my hands a little sweaty and my cheeks a little warmer. A quick glance at the clock, and it was fifteen minutes before Jarod would be here. By now, the two of us were sitting and sharing a meal during his Thursday visits, and sometimes Friday, too. We'd even split our own plate of fries, and laughed, dipping them in a milkshake we shared.

Tonight was an official date. Nothing fancy: a small dinner, and a movie. He said to dress casual, so I did. I found a cute white blouse, a bit puffy in the sleeves, though, and some jeans. The jeans were a newer style I saw the kids wearing, where the torn rips and the holes were normal: you *paid* for them. It still made no sense, but I bought the jeans, anyway. They made me look good. Really good. I even picked up a slick new pair of Chuck Taylor sneakers. Black. I loved them.

"You sure when he told you casual, this is what he meant by it?" Ms. Potts frowned, but with a smirk slipping through. Suzette walked around the counter, and punched her hips with her hands. She poked a foot out in a stance that was identical to one Ms. Potts liked to hold.

"I think she fine. Girl look fine," Suzette said in a playful mimic. When Ms. Potts pushed her eyes up and down in a study of Suzette, she blew up in a hearty laugh, clapping her hands together.

"Suzette got style – ya'll see her, she got style!" Ms. Potts laughed. Clark walked to the front, clapped a hand, turned to me, and added,

"M-Miss Gabby, you look beautiful. You surely do," he finished, and cautiously hugged me, on account of the white blouse. I appreciated that. The bell above the door echoed, and the four of us found Mr. Thurman coming in, carrying a set of what looked like legal documents.

"Well, look at you," he said. His eyes were bright and cheerful. I nodded and watched as he approached. When he joined our family at the counter, he looked to each one of us without saying a word. When I saw a tear dance in his eye and then fall, I reached out and put my hand on his arm.

"Mr. Thurmon, what is it?" He gave us all another look. A long look. He wasn't sad at all. He was happy.

"I'm going to miss you guys. Next to my own family, I come to think of you all as much a part of who I am. Especially you, Ms. Potts –"

"You stop that, now," Ms. Potts interrupted, "Junior, I want you to tell me what's going on," she demanded. Immediately, my heart sank, and I thought of the Asian men, the ones with the suits, who were buying Angela's and tearing our diner down. Clark and Ms. Potts were thinking it, too, as I watched their expressions turn to concern. I glimpsed the door, half expecting to see

Detective Ramiz walk through with a pair of handcuffs in hand, and sounding a bloody cough amidst a bellow of laughter.

But nothing happened. There were no police cars out front, or sounds of sirens, or blue lights shining through our windows and dancing across our ceiling. It was eerily quiet, and Mr. Thurmon stared a long time at Ms. Potts and Clark. He mouthed a thank you to them both, and then swiped the tear from his cheek.

A curious thing happened then. Suzette was smiling. In fact, she was beaming, and blurted a giggle. Before I could speak a word, she was bouncing up and down on her toes. Curious smiles were shared between Clark and Ms. Potts, while I started to laugh. I had no reason to. None at all. But the excitement caught me as Suzette hooped and hollered and bounced. Mr. Thurmon produced a set of keys, and dangled them in the middle of our little circle. He jostled and jiggled them so they rang out. He then explained that the keys were for the new owner.

"And now, meet the new owner of Angela's Diner: Miss Suzette!" He trumpeted, and handed her the keys. Our jaws dropped, and our eyes grew wide. Ms. Potts pulled her arms around Clark, and I could tell she was crying a relief that was twenty years in the waiting.

"But, how? How?" I asked, still shaking my head and laughing. Suzette continued bouncing, like one of those game show girls we'd seen from time and time on Clark's little TV.

"I had the money. I've always had the money: my *own* money. Just wasn't allowed to use it. Until now!" she answered, her voice pitched in excitement. And I realized there was so much more to her and her husband's story that I didn't know. I wondered if I would ever know, but then considered that it might be a story to be told over some coffee and tears. My arms fell over Suzette, and I pulled her close to me, and kissed her.

"You're the best," I whispered. "You saved them – you saved my family," I added, and then held her face in my hands, forehead to forehead.

"Gabby, don't you get it? You guys have been the only family I've had. Angela's is my home," she began to tear up, and then shook her hands, jingling the keys, and began to hop up and down again.

"Th-thank you, ma'am," Clark added, and kissed Suzette. Ms. Potts was speechless. She stood across from Suzette, her eyes fixed in a stare as she shook her head back and forth. Finally, she took Suzette's hands in hers, and kissed them. The ringing of the bell broke our quiet, and Mr. Thurmon moved to reveal Jarod. He stood with a same look of confusion that I guessed we'd had moments earlier.

"Suzette owns the diner now," Mr. Thurmon told him, giving him a slap on the back. Jarod raised a brow, and then turned to face Suzette. He stretched a hand with congratulations, and asked,

"Need a handyman?" Suzette lifted a finger to her chin, and formed a question in her eyes. She tapped her foot a few times, as if considering her options. When Jarod frowned, she answered in a laugh,

"Guys, nothing changes. I'm hoping you will all stay with me for as long as the diner is standing."

"But there *is* a change. We discussed it. In fact, it was your idea," Mr. Thurmon chided. Suzette lifted her face.

"You're right. I did make one change – the name is no longer Angela's, it's Suzette's."

"Suzette's is a lovely name," Ms. Potts exclaimed, and we all agreed, as a few of our regulars came up to congratulate her. My insides felt like Jell-O. A wash of nerves and giddiness played in a tug-o-war. I was happy.

"Don't you two have to be going?" Ms. Potts asked as she emerged from the group. Jarod repeated the question with his eyes. The diner was home, and, like most homes, there was change, good change. It was time for me to change again, too. I took Jarod's hand in mine, and stepped closer to him until we were inches apart.

"I know this is traditionally something you do at the end of a date, but I don't want to wait," I told him, and then pressed my mouth onto his, and gave him a long, hard kiss. He wrapped his arms around my middle, and kissed me back. When we were done I said,

"Now we can go." His face beamed with a grin. He then nodded to me, while lifting his hair from his eyes. I loved that he did that.

"Hey, boss," I yelled across the diner, "Can I take the night off?" Suzette turned and laughed.

"You bet, just come back for some desert later. And, if I pick up an order of coffee and tears, I'll be sure to share them with you."

Later the next day, we were hard at work for the three-to-three shift. The sound of metal on glass was a constant, as men out front busily scraped the name Angela's from the window. I felt a bittersweet tug in my heart as each of the letters disappeared forever.

The lettering of Angela's Diner was the first thing I noticed when I came upon what would become my home – well, that, and the smell of food. A memory bubble surfaced, and it was a good one. I saw my reflection in the glass of Angela's Diner. Staring back at me, I saw a young girl, a cold breath leaving her mouth in a whisper. She wore just the thinnest of clothing, a backpack hanging on her shoulder. She pegged the sidewalk with the tip of her Chuck Taylors, her heel wavering with pensive curiosity, as she looked over the diner for the first time. She was skinny, and hungry, and scared. And then her eyes opened wide. She'd found the help wanted sign in the window, and made a decision. It was a decision that changed her life forever.

"Well, you just going to stand there all day, or help out?" I heard Suzette's voice in my ear. Smiling, I turned to find her bright eyes, grinning and ready to take on the world – provided they were ordering up some food, that is.

When the bell above the door rang, I turned, and my breath was gone. It was my father. He'd come back to visit, but he wasn't alone. An older woman stood in front of him. She was small and round, and held familiar eyes on me. My legs turned wobbly, but I didn't want to run. My hands started to shake, and I felt both Suzette and Ms. Potts take a hold of my arms. My momma was here. She was here, at the diner, with my father. She was so much older. Older than ten years should have given her. A small pang of guilt pinched my heart, as I heard, "Be civil to your parents," echo in my head. It was my momma, and I fought the tears pressing in my eyes.

"Gonna be fine, Gabby," Ms. Potts said. "Go on now – go on to see your Momma."

In that moment, the pain and hurt of ten years went someplace, and I had no idea where that was. I missed my momma, and now she was standing just a few feet in front of me. Her eyes were wet, and she took a cautious step closer, raising a hand, as though she couldn't decide if this was real.

"Momma?" I cried, and clutched my hands together in front of me.

"Gabriella?" She yelled, and then pulled me into her arms. And I remembered everything about her. I remembered her voice, and her touch, and her smell. But more than anything, I remembered how I loved my momma. She pulled away just enough to look at my face, and then I heard her say,

"Mi Gabby, amo thee tan." I hadn't heard those words since I was a child. It was the only time she ever called me Gabby – she said, "My Gabby, I love thee so."

"I love you, too, Momma."

EPILOGUE

Soon after Angela's Diner came to be known as Suzette's Diner, I learned that Detective Ramiz had passed away. During a regular visit by *Keep on Truckin'*, he handed me the remains of his newspaper, where a photo of a younger Detective Ramiz was shown in a quarter page article. The detective was dressed in his full service uniform, and wore an expression that was decades younger than the dying face I'd come to know during his recent visits to the diner. Beneath his photo, the paper read his full name: Samuel Jonathan Ramiz. The paper also listed his accomplishments, and that he'd been survived by a wife, children, and grandchildren. That last accolade caught me off guard, and I realized that you really can't assume anything – Detective Ramiz was a person.

Suzette's Diner was a hit. The eventual closing of the

fast-food establishment helped. The article in the Philadelphia Magazine on Historic Restaurants was a pure windfall for her. Suzette was happier than I'd ever seen her, and she fell in love with being the owner of the diner. From time to time, Mr. Thurmon stopped in and sat at the counter, where I enjoyed his company. He'd watch Suzette and how she ran the diner. He'd say how much Suzette reminded him of his mother.

"She runs the diner with the same passion... the same love," he'd tell me. And he was right. Suzette found her love in owning and running the diner. She never married again, and, as far as I can remember, she never dated again. The diner became her life, and an order of coffee and tears became her own. Often times, I'd see her sitting with folks, sharing a cup of coffee, and counseling whatever was ailing them. She even closed the diner some evenings to hold closed meetings for battered women seeking help. I never attended any, but learned from dozens of grateful voices just how much Suzette had done for them. How much she'd changed their lives. I was so proud when I heard that.

We saw Mr. Thurmon less and less over the years. I was still a waitress at Suzette's when the news came that he died. The arthritis took his life years before any of us expected it would. We cried for him at the funeral, and, later that evening, we held a reception in the diner, where we celebrated his life. We drank and laughed, and told stories until the morning shift came in to prep for the next day.

It wasn't long after we lost Mr. Thurmon that a stroke took half of Clark. The entire right half of his body was paralyzed, leaving him to live out his remaining years in one of Philadelphia's finest retirement homes. Suzette made certain that Clark received the best room, the best care, and the best television, which tuned in episodes of Wheel of Fortune and Jeopardy every night.

Ms. Potts continued working at Suzette's well beyond her years. When she could no longer wait tables, Suzette offered her Angela's old place at the cash register. But Ms. Potts knew when her time was, and, with tears in her eyes, and a smile on her lips, she said it was her time to go. She retired to the same home where Clark lived his final years, and where Jarod, my husband, and I brought our two little ones to visit. *Grand-Mama*, they called her, and she called our children her own, just as she had with me years before. Nearing the age of ninety-five, Ms. Potts went to sleep one evening, and never woke up. She was found the next morning, holding a picture of all of us, taken years before in the diner. I'd like to think she died peaceful, with only good memories of Angela's. Her funeral was quiet and somber, and her death brought with it a kind of closure to the mystery of Angela's Diner.

For years, *Be civil to your parents* was something I continued to hear in my head; still do, in fact. And, so, I stayed civil, and began a new relationship with my parents. We talked almost every week, and made trips to and from Texas. You might even say we were normal. I never look back on the years we were apart. No need to. With the past behind me, I stay in today, since that is all we really have, anyway.

The lilting accent of Texans passing through one afternoon caught my ear. The sound of their voices tugged a string or two in my heart. The strings tugged some more when I had to tell them we didn't have any grits, or Texas-style red-beans and rice. Texas was home, and what I'd buried there stayed buried. But the voice of home got in my head, and in my heart. And, soon, the idea of home flourished the way ideas sometimes do. Before I realized it, I was asking Jarod if he was up for a move. He nodded with an excited smile, and we moved to the big state.

Today, we live in a town just a few miles from my parents. It is there that I started a new chapter in my life. I made a list of my own, and put it in Clark's old book, where I keep it on a shelf and read it from time to time. And, just like Clark said, you can always start over. So that is what we did.

Auntie Suzette visits a few times a year and always brings a bag full of Philadelphia with her. From soft-pretzels to cheese steaks and hoagies, packed in dry-ice, of course, Jarod is usually the first to greet her, digging into the bag of goodies. On one particular visit, I drove her out to an empty intersection, where an old abandoned boxcar eatery stood perched amidst long grass and grown out shrubs caught on the corners. The winds had blown Texas dust up along one side, so that the boxcar held tones of sandy brown and faded maroon.

Suzette winced at the sight of the boxcar, and asked why we were there. I held the keys up and jingled them in front of her. She nodded an understanding, and we went inside. There, she saw the work Jarod had already started. The boxcar was the front, and we were adding an entire addition, much like Angela Thurmon had done to Suzette's diner.

The boxcar diner was small, but I didn't mind. Gabby's Diner was going to be the first active boxcar restaurant our town had seen in more than fifty years. Suzette cheered and clapped her hands in front of her, and the image of it reminded me of Ms. Potts. I loved that she did that. She looked at me with a terrific grin on her face, and told me to get ready for more orders of coffee and tears.

THANK YOU

Thank you for reading *An Order of Coffee and Tears*.

If you liked *An Order of Coffee and Tears*, please take a moment to leave a review on Amazon. It would be *very* appreciated.

If you want to see what is coming up, or just read what I've jotted down, visit my site WrittenByBrian.

Look for some of my other novels and upcoming novels:

> Superman's Cape
>
> Glass Horses
>
> Fallen Pages
>
> Cradles In Prison
>
> The Sound
>
> Even Monsters Need Love
>
> The Devil Orders Takeout

ABOUT THE AUTHOR

A writer trapped in an Engineer's body, Brian Spangler was born in Philadelphia and enjoyed the greater Philadelphia area until career motivated a move south. Now living in Virginia with his wife and children along with three cats, a parrot, lizard, chinchilla, mouse and the occasional wild animal visiting late at night.

While growing up, a passion for writing was discovered that influenced many short stories, poems and song lyrics for that garage band that never made it on the radio.

Currently, Brian works as an Engineer and Enterprise Architect and enjoys time with family as well as reading and writing.

Made in the USA
Middletown, DE
20 October 2017